My Girlfriend Is a Werewolf

A Moonstruck Mating

Book One

Eve Langlais

INTRODUCTION

I've licked him. He's mine.

Running into a strange white wolf isn't an everyday occurrence in Derek's life. Neither is finding a naked—and beautiful—woman alone in the park. Had the wolf been an omen of what was yet to come? Because since meeting Athena, Derek's life's been upended.

Chased by thugs and with a ransom on her head, Athena isn't divulging why she's a wanted woman. Derek helps her anyway since he's a gentleman and she keeps his curiosity—and other things—piqued. Besides, he'll be damned if some greedy doctor is going to kidnap and experiment on innocent people in his own backyard.

But he can't help but notice Athena's great sense of smell, or her proclivity for chasing rabbits, or the way she disappears on the nights of the full moon...

INTRODUCTION

Turns out his Athena's got a hairy secret.

A howling whopper of one.

Guess he'd better stock up on flea collars and kibble because *My Girlfriend is a Werewolf*.

A MOONSTRUCK MATING IS PARANORMAL ROMANCE FEATURING 3 TITLES:

CHAPTER 1

THE FULL MOON WOULD BE RISING AFTER
dinner, which meant no more screwing around.
Athena needed out of her prison before anyone
confirmed her secret. She'd done well holding tight,
not giving into the anger when they spent hours
hosing her down with frigid water. She'd not barked
once when they forced her to spend time with cats or
someone delivered something to her cell. The sirens
they played had her tempted to howl, but she bit her
tongue.

Pretending to be a normal human being took its
toll, but she'd managed thus far. However, Athena
couldn't do anything about the blood and tissue
samples the various technicians took. At least she could
be comforted with the fact a few weird chromosomes
didn't mean shit without proof of what that special
twist in her DNA meant.

1

But she wouldn't be able to hide her secret tonight.

A week of flirting with her afternoon guard would hopefully pay off. She needed to escape before they trotted her outside and exposed her to moonlight—the one thing she couldn't resist.

Simon, the guy on shift, arrived with her meal tray, and Athena offered him a simpering smile as he brought it into her cell. He no longer gave her the daily warning to stand in the far corner. Her ploy to fool him into thinking her harmless appeared to be working.

As Simon set down her dinner, she murmured, "Thanks. You take such good care of me." Athena batted her lashes so hard they almost took flight.

"Just doing my job." Simon hitched his pants by the loops and puffed his barrel chest. A thick fellow, but she'd tussled with bigger.

"Guess after tonight we won't see each other anymore once they realize I'm not what they think I am." Her lips turned down in feigned sadness.

"You could call me when you're released," he offered. "We could go to dinner and stuff."

"If only that were possible. Given what I know about this facility, I fear what they'll do to me." She ducked her head as she played the melodramatic damsel.

"I'm sure Dr. Rogers won't do anything drastic. Mistakes happen."

Of course, Simon would defend the doctor who'd

been the one to trap her and organize the tests. Everyone in this installation worshipped Dr. Rogers, the man who'd caught the first Sasquatch. The guy who'd proved the existence of Ogopogo while also disproving Nessie using some kind of deep sonar tech. And now Dr. Rogers planned to out lycanthropes.

She still had no idea how he'd sniffed out her existence. Athena always took great care to never be seen when she ran on four feet.

"I hope you're right and this is all a big misunderstanding, but what if this is my last moment on Earth?" She clutched her chest. "What if my last kiss was that slobbery one by that drunk in a bar? If only I had a nicer memory to take with me."

Simon blinked, and it took his pea-sized brain a second to figure out what she hinted at.

"Uh, er..." He glanced at the camera in the cell with its red blinking light.

Someone always watched and listened. It took everything in her to be as boring as possible. Lying on her cot counting the dots in the ceiling tile. Staring off blankly into space. When she couldn't stand to be sedentary, she'd do push-ups or jumping jacks but not so many as to seem suspicious.

They must be wondering by now if they'd assumed wrong since she'd not once peed in a corner nor wagged her butt in excitement when her dinner came with dessert.

"I'm sorry. I shouldn't have even asked. I'm just so

scared! It's so unfair. I didn't do anything," she exclaimed and grabbed the pudding—chocolate, her favorite—and threw it. Her aim proved good, as it hit the camera and gooey goodness smothered the lens, ruining their eyes and hopefully muffling their ears. She wouldn't have long.

"Oh shit," Simon muttered, eyeing the mess.

She grabbed him by the shirt. "Quick, kiss me before they come."

"Uh…"

What a meathead. Would she have to do everything?

A mash of her mouth to Simon's distracted as she divested him of the notepad in his back pocket, where she knew he kept the door codes written because Simon couldn't remember the many-numbered sequences. She'd been carefully scouting which of the guards she could use in her escape, and Simple Simon won hands-down.

As Simon began to moan, she suddenly shoved him in the direction of the cot. The backs of his legs hit it, and he fell hard. Bemused, he didn't immediately clue in that she'd exited to the hall, but he started yelling when she slammed the cell door shut.

Step one, get out of her room. Done.

She ran up the hall, bare feet slapping the cold tile. The next door had a keypad. She flipped open the notebook and could have cursed at the sloppy writing.

Simon had several entries; Main, Pretty Girl, Ugly Dude. Hall 1, Hall 2, Stairs, Yard.

Which one to use? When Hall 1 didn't work, she cursed and quickly punched Hall 2. As the door clicked and she yanked it open, an alarm went off.

Things were about to get dicey. Usually her favorite kind.

The next hall held a woman in a lab coat carrying a tablet. Dr. Lanier, the psychologist who'd been trying to trick Athena into admitting her furry side.

As if. Athena had been taught from a young age to never ever say a thing. Daddy might be gone now, but his lessons remained.

"What are you doing out of your cell?" Dr. Lanier squeaked.

"Blowing this joint. I'd say nice knowing you, but that would be a lie," Athena grumbled as she barreled for the woman. Lanier did nothing to stop her, unless screeching, "Help!" counted.

The shoulder Athena used to ram the doctor aside proved satisfying. Not as satisfying as, say, biting her, but Athena didn't have time for revenge. Plotting retaliation would come later.

If she escaped.

The next keypad unlocked the door the moment she punched in the code for the stairs. It opened onto a staircase and elevator. Since the numbers showed it coming down, she fled up the steps and ran into a pair of soldiers descending. Her momentum let her drive into their legs and send them tumbling. She continued her bolt upwards, only to stop in surprise at the first-floor landing.

Dr. Rogers stood there waiting for the elevator. A pair of armed guards flanked the tall man with his wire-rimmed glasses, bowtie, and customary white coat. The guards aimed their revolvers at Athena.

Dr. Rogers yelled, "Don't shoot to kill. We need her alive."

A fellow with an impressive mustache said, "So aim for a leg or an arm?"

Their hesitation gave Athena the chance she needed. She roundhouse-kicked the gun out of one hand and followed with an uppercut to the second guy. As they reeled in surprise, a left hook plus a right cross laid another two other guards flat out. *Thank you, Daddy, for the lessons and increased strength.* Athena might not look it, but she could pack a punch.

The doctor didn't look impressed she'd taken out his security. "There is no escape. Even if you make it out of the facility, I will find you."

"You're assuming I won't find you first," she chirped. "I'll be seeing you..." She waved as she slammed through the door that led to the lobby. A lobby full of armed guards who eyed her in shock.

As guns left holsters, the doctor saved her again. "Don't you dare use those weapons. Someone fetch the tranquilizer guns."

Since the lobby area had too many even for her to

slam through, Athena ran the other way, heading for the door that led to the yard. Dr. Rogers had been having her escorted to it nightly as the moon got fatter and fatter.

'Yard' proved to be a bit of a misnomer. It was a concrete space surrounded by barbed-wire fencing. Beyond it, a line of trees thick enough to prevent casual passersby from spying. Wouldn't the folks in Ottawa be surprised to know the Experimental Farm wasn't just about testing crops? Their basement level hosted a lab for other things.

The fencing with its sharp tines would hurt, but Athena preferred a bit of pain to being incarcerated and outed. However, to give herself the best chance, the shirt came off, and as she ran, she tore the thin fabric of the scrub top to wrap around her hands. The barbed metal still bit her flesh, but she gritted her teeth and climbed, even as she could hear the commotion at her back.

Despite expecting to be shot—probably in the ass with her luck—she kept ascending.

"Shoot the darts!" Dr. Rogers screamed. "Quick. She's about to escape."

Indeed, she was. Freedom beckoned, but she'd be cutting it close. Blame Simon for arriving later than usual. Twilight would shortly descend, and that meant the pull of the moon was strong as it began to rise in the coming night sky.

Athena hit the ground on the other side of the

fence with a grunt and a bend of the knees. A good thing she'd ducked as a dart whizzed over her head, the soldier having gotten lucky and shot it through the diamond-shaped holes in the fence.

Her bare feet pounded the ground as she took off running, immediately heading for the woods where she could use the shadows and branches to make it harder for them to aim.

As she sprinted, her skin began tingling in warning. She gritted her teeth against it. Not yet. She needed to be out of sight, not only of human eyes but electronic ones.

As she burst from the tree line, moonlight hit, and she couldn't fight it anymore. No lycanthrope could. The change came quickly, not a magical transition from human to wolf, but also not the violent tearing that Netflix portrayed in *Hemlock Grove*. More like seconds of joint popping, skin shivering, and senses muffled before she hit the ground on four paws.

Athena ran. Ran faster than the shouting soldiers chasing her.

The problem then became, where to go?

Home was out of the question, as was hitting up her friends or family. She had no money for a motel. So what did that leave?

Hours later, she still had no clue, until she saw the jogger being accosted and joined the fight.

CHAPTER 2

DEREK BROWSED HIS LOCAL REDDIT FOR NEWS as he waited for the elevator in his apartment building. Mostly the same old thing.

Why are people so rude these days?

OMG rent is outrageous.

And then a new one...

White wolf sighted along Rideau Canal. And within the last hour, too.

He snorted. More likely a large dog or a coyote. Ontario had wolves, but they tended to stay far from big cities like Ottawa.

As the bell dinged and the elevator door slid open, he tucked his phone into the armband he wore for jogging. He probably should have taken the stairs down, but the last time, someone had pissed in the stairwell, and he'd stepped in it. Those shoes got tossed. It was one thing to piss on his own shoes because he was drunk and lacked aim, another to slosh around in someone else's urine.

As Derek exited his building, he broke into a light jog. Fall, his favorite time of year. The evenings got dark early, the air crisp instead of redolent like in summer with the festering garbage. Even better, fewer people on the trails running along the river so he could jog without having to play dodge the pedestrian. Then again, not many people out and about this time of night. He'd worked a graveyard shift, getting off at four instead of one since someone failed to show, home by five because transit sucked. Despite the hour, he liked to indulge in a quick jog then be in bed by dawn so he could get up early afternoon to do it again. Not ideal, but rent needed to be paid.

He might not have minded his dull life so much if he at least had a girlfriend. His last one hadn't worked out. Apparently, after six months of dating, him saying "We should move in together" was controlling. According to Stacy, "You're stifling me. I need my space." It should be noted they saw each other maybe once a week, given their alternating schedules. The whole let's-live-together thing had been his way of spending more time with her since she'd also complained, "I never see you."

At thirty-three, Derek could safely say he didn't understand women, but that didn't deter him. As his grams always said, "There's a bitch out there somewhere, you little bastard. So chin up, make sure to wash your bits, and whatever you do, don't tell them you like pineapple on pizza." Because, according to his grandma, women would run screaming if they knew.

Grams tended to tell things straight with many cuss words. It made school concerts growing up entertaining because Grandma had no problem hollering, *"Sit your ass down. Some of us want to see something other than your talentless jizz."* Also amusing? Her ranting as the refs tossed her out of his hockey games for taunting the opposing team. Then there was the grilling of Derek's potential GF's with questions like, *"Can you cook, or is your idea of fine dining opening a can?" "You going to be true to my grandson, or am I gonna have to take you out to the woodshed for a chat?"* His favorite... *"So what prepping have you done for the apocalypse?"* For some reason, that question sent a few running. Good. Derek didn't need someone who would question his stockpile of water, Ramen noodles, and his bug-out bag for when shit hit the fan.

He'd yet to meet a woman who passed the Grams test, although a few, after meeting her, did think they could demand he cut her out of his life. Like fuck. *Love me, love my family.*

Heavy metal blasted in his air pods, the heavy beat the perfect accompaniment for the slap of his sneakers on pavement. The lights along the canal lit the path well until a section by a bench overlooking the water.

Burnt out or vandalized? Probably the latter. Since the pandemic, crime had gotten worse.

Speaking of which, as he entered the dark section, three dudes wearing face masks, bulky hoodies, and oozing attitude stepped into his path.

Derek slowed his jog and drawled, "Morning, fellas." Because with dawn about to burst, it was no longer night.

"Give us your stuff." The skinniest one held out his hand.

Derek arched a brow. "I'd rather not. I hate setting up new phones."

"Hand it over or else," a second dude ordered, whipping out a switchblade.

It led to Derek eyeballing guy number three. "Let's hear it. Don't let your buddies get all the threatening glory."

"Uh..." Guy number three apparently didn't have a catch phrase of his own.

"Okay boys, let's get this done." It should be noted, Grams didn't just teach him how to swear more mightily than a trucker—and she could get quite creative when it came to cussing at drivers that should get out of her fucking way. Grams had been in her fair share of bar fights because she did so love her whiskey, but if she mixed it with beer... watch out.

To those who might be appalled he'd taken pugilistic lessons from a little old lady, one, his grandma wasn't little, and two, she'd never lost a fight—something Gramps took pride in. Gramps liked to sit back and watch, even wager, and had won more than a few tidy sums that way.

"Guess we're doing this the hard way." The guy with the knife took one step forward, and Derek almost rolled his eyes.

"Dude, did no one ever teach you how to use that thing?" Derek reached out, chopped the wrist, and grabbed the falling blade. "Let's get rid of this before you cut yourself." He pulled back his arm and tossed the flimsy weapon into the flowing water.

Three sets of surprised eyes ogled him before guy number one barked, "Get him!"

Three against one. Looked like he'd be getting a full cardio workout tonight.

Sweet!

Derek ducked under a clumsy blow and nailed the guy in the diaphragm, bending him over double. He then spun and thumped the dumb one, clocking him in the face and sending him reeling.

Number three would have turned and run, only a giant white dog stood in their way, growling softly, hackles raised. Must be the wolf they were talking about on Reddit.

Derek ignored the pup as he grabbed the men he'd smacked and tossed them into the canal. Let the water wash away their sins. Or drown them. Either way, a win for society.

Guy number three apparently had a knife of his own, and he pulled it to threaten the big floof.

"Out of my way, mutt." Thief number three feinted with his blade, and the big dog looked unimpressed.

Derek, however, took exception. "Animal abuse is not cool, dude. Pick on someone human."

The guy half turned to snarl, "Fuck off, or I'll stab you too."

"Have you learned nothing in the last two minutes?" With that, Derek kicked the back of buddy's knee and, before the guy could recover, chopped the hand with the knife. *Plop*. The weapon went for a swim and drowned.

"What the fuck, man?" whined the dude.

"Listen up because I am about to give you some really good life advice. One, stop robbing hard-working folk. I don't bust my ass forty-plus hours a week for some lazy pukes to steal my shit. Get a fucking job. Two, three against one? Not cool, dude. If you wanna have a go at someone, then it's one-on-one. And ditch the knife. If you're gonna fight, then do so like a man. Three, if you're going to play tough guy, then can you at least take some lessons? This was pathetic. I didn't even break a sweat."

Derek would have sworn the dog appeared amused as it cocked its head. The wannabe thief was more confused than anything.

"Are you a cop?"

Derek actually shuddered. "Fuck no. Just a regular Joe who isn't fucking about to let three punks bully him. Now, I'll give you a choice. Jump or get tossed."

"What?"

"Jesus you're stupid. I blame our public education system." Derek reached over and grabbed the guy, hauling him off his feet before heaving him over the railing to join his friends, who clung to the concrete side of the canal blubbering about it being cold. He leaned over the rail to give them one final piece of advice. "Don't let me see you again."

With that, he turned to the dog. "Hey, puppers. You lost? Hungry?" He didn't see a collar.

The dog, a good size, with a fluffy coat of white fur, glanced to the sky, which began to lighten, before yipping and running off. Probably had to get home before its owner realized it had gone missing.

Derek pressed play on his phone and resumed his jog, only to pause about a hundred yards later when a naked woman jumped out from behind a tree.

Startled, he just about fell over. He also had to tuck his tongue into his mouth because holy hot babe.

Platinum hair that was almost silvery white, honey-colored skin, peach-sized boobs, narrow waist, and, damn, the carpet matched the drapes.

He gaped, at a rare loss for words.

Her lips moved, but it took him a second to flip off his music and mutter, "Say that again?"

"I need help. I've been robbed."

15

So not a drug addict in the midst of an episode. Had to watch for those. Nothing worse than being accosted by a naked woman wielding a knife who screamed she collected dicks. And, yes, it had happened. Grams gave him shit when she found out he fled. *"Why didn't you take her down?" "Because I wasn't about to have a sexual assault charge on my permanent record."* These days instigators somehow got away with being victims.

"You need me to call the cops and an ambulance?" Derek asked the woman. He went to dial 911, and she exclaimed, "Oh fuck no. I don't need to answer a zillion questions or have some paramedics groping me. I'm fine. Just naked."

A reminder that had him stripping his long-sleeve Henley. "Here take this. Sorry, it's a bit sweaty from my jog."

She didn't seem to care as she slid it over her head, covering those luscious curves.

Mmm-hmm.

And what the fuck was wrong with him? This woman had been attacked. He shouldn't be looking at her lustily at all. If Grams were here, she'd have cuffed him for sure.

"Thanks," the beautiful woman murmured.

"Can I call someone for you?"

She shook her head. "No."

"Need a ride? I can call a cab and get them to drop you off at your place."

Her teeth worried her lower lip before she admitted, "I don't remember where I live."

"You have amnesia?" He couldn't help sounding incredulous.

"Seems so." She shrugged.

"You really should go to a hospital if you got smacked in the head."

"No doctors," she scowled. "I'm more hungry than hurt."

Not the reply he expected. "Do you need me to buy you some food?"

"Depends, know any places doing steak this time of day?" A fleeting smile curved her perfect lips.

"Not around here."

"Pity. A good steak, barely singed, always fixes everything."

A woman after his own heart. "Well, guess I should get going, that is unless you've changed your mind about me calling a cab."

"Can't I just go home with you? I just need a place to crash for a day or two."

And here came the grift. Derek pursed his lips. "Listen, lady, I don't do scams, and before you deny it, I know how this works. I take you to my place. Next thing I know, some gorilla shows up claiming to be your boyfriend. He beats the crap out of me, and you rob me blind."

Her lips parted. "Does that actually happen?"

"Not to me, but I read about it on Reddit."

EVE LANGLAIS

"So that's a no on a place to crash for a few days?"

"Guess you'll have to amnesia-scam someone else."

She sighed. "Bloody hell. As you might have guessed, I don't have amnesia, but I can't go home. It's not safe."

"Then why not say that in the first place?" Derek crossed his arms and gave her a stern look.

"Because I'm not looking for a hero. Just somewhere to hang while I figure shit out."

"There are shelters you know."

"The second place they'll look," she muttered.

"What's the first?"

"My apartment."

Her answers had him frowning. "Who's looking for you?"

"Some bad folks. I need to lie low for a while until I know it's safe, and before you ask, I don't have money for a motel. I can't contact my family or friends, not if I want to keep them safe. What a fucking clusterfuck."

Look at her using Grams' favorite word. While Derek got the impression the naked lady wasn't telling the whole truth, he didn't get a danger vibe from her. On the contrary, he found himself intrigued, and it wasn't as if he couldn't take care of himself. If a goon showed up, he'd show him a lesson about what happened to scum who preyed on good Samaritans.

"You know what, you can come stay for a few days, but I warn you—I've got only one bed, and it's mine."

18

Because his chivalry only went so far. "You're welcome to the couch, though."

"Couch is fine. I've slept on worse."

"Follow me, then."

As they began to walk, he asked, "What's your name?"

"Athena."

"As in the goddess?"

"Yeah. My mom loved the Greek gods. I'm Athena, and I have a brother called Ares, and a sister named Selene."

"I'm Derek, after my gramps." Idle chitchat, kind of incongruous given he walked with an almost naked hottie. He noticed her bare feet. "Do you need me to carry you?"

"Whatever for? My legs work."

"Because you have no shoes and I don't want you cutting your feet or something."

She glanced at her toes. "Bah. I'll be fine."

Tough chick. Most broads would have been in hysterics after being robbed. Or... "Wait, were you actually robbed?"

"Not exactly. More like kidnapped and held prisoner."

"By who?"

"Some very annoying people," she grumbled. "When my chance came to escape, I didn't have time to get dressed. Guess I'm lucky the first person I came across wasn't a rapist."

"Fuck those pervs. Grams says the only way to cure a rapist is to cut off his dick and choke him with it."

A short laugh emerged from her. "I like your grandma already."

"You'd be one of a few," he admitted ruefully. "She scares off most folks."

"Not you?" she questioned.

"Nah. She's awesome. I hope to be half as tough as her one day."

They reached his apartment building, an ugly thing built back in the seventies. Red brick with no character. He unlocked and held open the door for her to enter the vestibule. She angled her head and sniffed before saying, "Is there a building in this city that doesn't have pee in the stairwells?"

She could smell it in the lobby? Might be time to ask the superintendent to bleach the stairs again. "Yeah, it's getting to be bad in a lot of places. At least the rent isn't horrendous."

"Oh don't apologize. Just pointing out a fact. My place had the same problem for a bit."

"How did you solve it?"

"The pisser had an unfortunate tumble down the stairs and landed face first in it."

He couldn't help but laugh. "By unfortunate, do you mean pushed?"

"Why, Derek, do I look like the type of girl who would sully her hands?" Athena drawled then winked.

He kept chuckling as they entered the elevator.

"Kind of refreshing to meet someone who doesn't put up with bullshit. Although I gotta wonder, how did you get involved in a bad scene?"

"By not being careful." She leaned against the elevator wall as it rose. "And before you ask, I'd never met the folks who snagged me. All I know is apparently I met some kind of criteria."

Given her looks, he could only come to one conclusion. Sex trafficked. Damn. Meaning no flirting by him, no leering, no nothing. Derek wasn't about to make her trauma greater.

"Think they'll come looking for you?"

"Probably." She hesitated before adding, "Don't worry. I'll be gone before they figure out where I am."

She kept saying "they." As in, more than one person.

"Even if they do show up, I'm not afraid," he quickly stated. "More just wondering if I need to be more on guard than usual."

"You should be fine. It's me they're after."

"Any way I can help you get them off your back?" he offered, because his grandma raised him to be a gentleman who helped people in need. And he hated scum. If vigilante justice wasn't punished more severely than actual criminals, he'd have long ago started cleaning up the city.

"You've already done enough by giving me a place to crash for a few days. Thanks."

"No problem."

With that, they arrived at his place. She declared the couch perfect, and then, despite his earlier claim, Derek tried to insist she take the bed because he suddenly felt bad about putting her on that lumpy thing. She refused.

He might have fought longer, but he needed sleep before his shift tonight. He pulled out some leftovers in the fridge, a bucket of fried chicken and another of hot wings which they devoured in silence—unless her staring meant something. After their meal, he said goodnight and hoped he wouldn't wake to an apartment stripped of all his valuables. He'd be pissed if she took his collector edition Xbox.

CHAPTER 3

ATHENA LAY ON THE COUCH LISTENING AS Derek actually went to bed and slept. Slept with a slight snore, despite the stranger in his place. Was he nuts? Then again, she'd seen him in action on the path by the canal. The guy knew how to handle himself.

At first, when she'd seen him confronted by those three thugs, she'd expected him to get beaten. Her plan had been to snag his keys, find out his address by stealing his wallet back from the bullies—along with a shirt since dawn wasn't far off—and then head to his place for a few hours of rest while he got handled at the hospital, which these days took upwards of eight hours, sometimes closer to twenty-four.

Only that plan failed before it began since Derek disarmed the would-be thieves but not in a violent way. He literally chastised them instead of beating them silly. He was much nicer than her. She even tested his nice streak by appearing naked and asking for help. Had he turned into a pig, she would have beaten his ass and kept to her initial plan, but he'd proven to be a gentleman, offering her his shirt, showing caution at her asking to stay, then actually being a nice guy by offering her his bed and, when she said no, a clean T-shirt, boxers, and a blanket with pillow.

He'd not once tried to grope her. Kept his gaze on her face and not once made any kind of sexual innuendo. She'd have thought him into men if she'd not seen his expression light up when he'd first seen her.

At least now she could stop running and rest for a bit. She'd spent the night racing around the city, muddying any trail she left, hopefully foiling anyone trying to follow. She'd not once thought of popping by her place because Dr. Rogers probably had people watching it the moment she escaped. Asshole.

Soon as she could get her hands on a phone, she would need to get in contact with her family, who most likely worried. She tended to talk to them several times a week. That was assuming Rogers hadn't taken them into custody and kept them in a different location, which didn't seem likely given his elaborate lab setup. Good thing they lived about an hour west of the city. It might have kept them safe, at least while Rogers still tried to ascertain her lycanthropy.

She couldn't be sure if her wolf was spotted in the escape. In either case, her family needed warning, but

MY GIRLFRIEND IS A WEREWOLF

she couldn't use Derek's phone. If Rogers already surveilled her family, then he'd trace it the moment she called. She'd have to get a burner phone and run her call through a VPN to make it seem like she was elsewhere.

As to how she'd get the money to buy it...

Rather than steal from her host, she prepared to offer him a deal when he woke. A yawning Derek emerged from the bedroom at one p.m., wearing low-slung track pants, a form-fitting faded T, and ruffled hair. He waved as he walked by the couch, muttering, "Afternoon."

An already awake Athena listened to the news on low. She turned to watch him in the tiny kitchen preparing a coffee.

"Good afternoon to you too. You slept good?" she asked.

"Like a cat."

She blinked. "Isn't the expression baby?"

"Grams says that's the stupidest thing ever since they sleep like shit most of the time. Cats, though, they know how to get some shuteye," he offered with a grin. He held up a mug. "Shot of caffeine?"

"Yes, please."

He also pulled out a box of cereal and milk, along with two bowls, and put them on his small kitchen table.

"I gotta go to work around three. Need anything

before I go? You're welcome to any clothes in my closet or food in the kitchen."

She hesitated before saying, "I need a hundred bucks."

"Okay." He said nothing else, so she added, "I'll pay you back soon as I can."

He glanced at her. "I assume this isn't for drugs."

"Hell no. I want to grab a prepaid phone."

"You could borrow mine."

"I'd prefer something anonymous."

He arched a brow. "Are you a spy being tracked by the government?"

"And if I was?"

His lips curved. "So long as you're not trying to take down Canada, it's cool."

She couldn't help but laugh. "I promise nothing so nefarious. But I'd like to be cautious so the assholes who took me don't know where I am."

His expression darkened. "How badly did they hurt you?"

"Nothing I couldn't handle. I'm more pissed about the situation than anything."

"Were you sex trafficked?" He sounded hesitant asking.

The query rounded her mouth. "No, although I could see why'd you think that, given my state of deshabille."

Once more, his low baritone laugh rang out,

26

sending a shiver through her. "Who the fuck uses deshabille in conversation?"

"A girl whose mother bought her a calendar that featured a new word for each day of the year."

"My calendar had half-naked girls because Gramps said those were the only acceptable calendars for a boy."

"And your grandma was okay with it?"

"Grams was the one who bought it."

Now it was her turn to laugh. "I kind of want to meet her."

"You sure you didn't hit your head?" he quizzed.

The giggle was so unlike her, and yet this man... he kept surprising her. "My family's a little strange too." Understatement. Selene, also a wolf, raised rabbits. Loved them to death. Literally. She let a few loose each full moon for sport while selling others to restaurants. Athena's brother, Ares, had a thing for cheese. Made it artisan-style from goat's milk. Unlike Selene, though, his wolf didn't eat the animals he raised. He preferred to go after the coyotes that harassed the family farm. Their mom seemed kind of normal in comparison, given she sold honey and country pies.

"Your coffee, milady." Derek handed her a mug of steaming java and sat down to eat his cereal. She joined him and studied him over the rim of her mug.

"Go on, ask," he mumbled around a mouthful of Honeycomb.

"Ask what?"

"Whatever question is brewing in your intense stare."

"You're being awfully nice considering you don't know a thing about me."

"You were a naked woman asking for help. Only an asshole would have walked away."

"Aren't you curious at all about me and my situation?"

He eyed her. "Would you tell me the truth if I asked?"

"I can't."

"Then no point in poking."

"How old are you?" she queried.

"Thirty-three. You?"

"Twenty-nine."

"I thought you were younger," his reply as he spooned more cereal.

"You're single?" She'd seen no sign of a woman in his place, nor smelled any. "Just wondering if I'm going to have someone screaming at me if they come over and find me here."

"Not seeing anyone, but not by choice. Still waiting for the right chick to come along."

"If you call her chick, she might not stay."

He leaned back in his chair, which creaked. The mismatched set looked to be on its last legs. "I come from a no-filter family who doesn't do any of this modern woke-language shit. Meaning anyone I do end up with has to be able to handle me using words like fuck, shit, dude, and chick. I mean, hell, my grams calls me the little bastard since my mom and dad never married, and before you get offended, she loves me. I'm the apple of her eye, so it's more like a term of endearment."

"Fair enough. I get you wanting to be you, and your family is obviously important."

"Very. So love me, love my cussing grandma and my cigarette-smoking Gramps."

"And your parents?"

"Bethany left when I was a kid. Wasn't cut out to be a mom. Dad's still kicking around. He works in construction."

"What about you?"

"Volunteer firefighter and, in my off time, warehouse worker."

Well, that explained the muscles. "So you're good with a hose and handling boxes." She said it deadpan, and he choked on his coffee.

She smiled as she sipped hers.

He wiped the mess and eyed her. "That was naughty."

"Who me?" Innocently said with a devilish smile.

Amusement curved his lips. "You're something else."

"Says the guy with interesting design tastes."

"Can't take the credit. The place came fully furnished. I basically just moved in my clothes."

"Handy. Lived here long?"

He shook his head. "A few months now. Grams told me to get my ass out of her house. Said I needed a social life outside the farm."

"Kind of the same reason I left ours too. Only I'm not so good at the whole making-friends thing. Sometimes I miss the chaos of having family underfoot all the time. Although I'd never admit to them I'm lonely."

"I hear you." Silence fell before he said, "I gotta shower before work since I skipped it after my jog. Need the bathroom first?"

"Go ahead."

He stood but before he headed to his only washroom grabbed some money from the cookie jar on his counter. "Here's two hundred in case you need extra for the phone and other stuff. There's more if you need some. I'm afraid I don't have any girly stuff here like tampons and whatnot."

Her turn to almost choke. Most men never used the T word. "You're being too nice."

"I better be, or Grams will whoop my ass." He winked and went to shower, leaving her to ponder this enigma of a man. Here she'd been prepared to offer him a blowjob for cash, and he'd just tossed it at her.

She would pay him back, plus some, soon as she got Rogers to stop hunting her.

Restless, Athena prowled his living space, inspecting it more thoroughly. He showered quicker than expected. If he thought it odd to find her ass up, face under his couch, where much could be told about a person, he said nothing.

She popped out and said, "Nice gun you got under there."

"Grams got it for me," he said, not a bit nonplussed by her snooping. "I'm heading out now for work. There's a spare house and vestibule key on the rack by the door."

"What time will you be home?"

"Around two if I don't get fucked by no-shows at work and my bus."

"Have a great day, honey," she chirped.

He snorted. "You too, sugarplum."

She found herself grinning and shaking her head as he left.

Left her alone in his space.

The level of trust baffled. Then again, with her upbringing, everything seemed suspicious. Neighbor came knocking to say hello, Mom assumed they were being nosy. A car drove down their country road, and it had to be someone surveilling. In Mom's defense, she worried about her kids. All three lycanthropes. Just like their dad, a man dead in his prime because someone shot him when he was out running during a full moon.

Unlike legends, the whole werewolf thing didn't come via a bite or a virus. From what Athena had gleaned, it occurred at a genetic level, meaning you were either born with it or not. And it sometimes skipped a kid. Dad's brother never got it, but his sister did.

Thinking of her family had her readying herself to go out. A shower was welcome, as was a scrub of her teeth with a finger and toothpaste. Delaying, but then again, a few extra minutes wouldn't make a difference, given it had been weeks since she'd talked to them. God only knew what they thought.

Derek's clothes hung loosely on her, which worked to conceal her figure. The ball cap hid her hair, and his sunglasses worked to cover her face. While Ottawa didn't have a CCTV network like Britain, there were enough cameras watching that she worried Rogers and his vast resources would still be able to track her. She'd seen a show about how they could tap into security cameras and use a computer program to scan for specific faces.

It took a few blocks of walking—and glancing over her shoulder often, checking to see if anyone stared overly long—before she found a store with prepaid phones. On her way back to the apartment, her neck constantly prickling, despite no one seeming to pay her any mind, she hit the Salvation Army for some clothes and then a pharmacy for a toothbrush and other essentials. By the time she retraced her steps to Derek's building, her pace rapid, as she felt exposed, she had three dollars and eleven cents left.

She dumped it into his cookie jar and made a note

beside it how much she owed. A McMurray, like a Lannister, always paid their debts.

As she chewed on a buttered and toasted bagel, she got the prepaid phone ready, downloading an app that would allow her to call as well as set her location to wherever she liked. She chose Montreal. If Rogers monitored her family's phone, then he'd think she fled the province.

It took a few deep breaths before she rang her mom.

"Hello, you've reached Beatrice's Honey Bee Emporium, how can I help you?" chirped her mother.

"Hey, Mom."

Dead silence.

"Mom?"

"OHMYGAWD!" Mom wailed. "I thought you were dead!"

"I'm not, but I might be deaf," Athena muttered, holding the burner phone away from her head.

"Where have you been? Why haven't you called?" Mom kept screeching.

"I kind of got kidnapped by an evil doctor who was convinced something was wrong with me." A roundabout, but also to the point, way of telling what happened. If anyone listened, she'd not revealed anything, but Mom would understand.

A deep silence ended when her mom whispered, "Shit." For a woman who never swore, it just went to show how hard the news hit.

"Are Selene and Ares okay?" Athena closed her eyes as she waited for a reply.

"Yes, but Ares says someone's been watching our place the last couple of weeks."

The blood in Athena's veins turned cold. "Please tell me they've been careful." Both her siblings loved to shift and run in the moonlight.

"They've barely left the house since you went missing. It was all I could do to keep them here instead of heading into the city to hunt you down. Good thing Barbara June told us you were okay." Barbara June, their closest neighbor and a bit of a psychic. She made money reading people's futures and was one of the few who knew their secret. Knew because the spirits told her. "Where are you? Is it safe?"

"I'm okay for now. I'm staying with a friend."

"When are you coming home?"

She closed her eyes and sighed. "I don't know." Left unsaid: it would be too dangerous.

"I miss you, baby girl."

"Miss you too, Mom." Her throat tightened. She had to protect her family. Especially now. With Rogers having lost Athena, would he go after them next? "Are you guys still going on that trip to visit Uncle George?"

They had no Uncle George, but the oblique reference acted as a clue, and Mom caught on.

"Well, we were going to wait for you to go. You know he loves seeing all you kids."

"Can't get away at the moment but give him my love."

"Will do, baby girl. Love you."

"Love you, too."

She hung up and took a deep breath then another. At least now she knew her family hadn't gotten caught up in the Rogers mess. Not yet. Hopefully Mom would have Selene and Ares packed and hiked out into the bush by the end of the day. Because what better way to foil watchers than to disappear in the wilds? They used to do it all the time growing up, Dad wanting them to learn how to live off the land just in case. They'd nicknamed the hut deep in the wilds Uncle George's place. It became a running joke with them saying they were going to visit their uncle when they needed to blow off some steam.

With her family taken care of, time to plan her next move.

Rogers needed taking down, which meant locating him. Preferably at home. Only he wasn't listed anywhere she looked. No phone number or address, just the news reports featuring him when he went viral for his amazing finds.

As she stared at the picture of Rogers standing beside the Sasquatch in a cage, her lips pursed. That had almost been her. The whole world had been only hours away from finding out werewolves really existed. Sometimes she wished she didn't have to hide. That she could be loud and proud about her heritage.

How bad would it be?

Just ask Fred, the Bigfoot who'd been put on display in Calgary and became a huge tourist attraction. He'd lost weight and hair since his captivity. Poor guy. At least the Ogopogo got to stay in its lake, albeit under guard.

Athena would die if they ever served her up like a circus freak.

She had to make sure that never happened.

Even if she had to kill her first human to do so.

CHAPTER 4

DEREK HATED HIS JOB. MONOTONOUS, repetitive, and long. So very long. He kept eyeballing the huge clock over the exit. He didn't usually pay it much mind, but thoughts of Athena kept intruding. Had she left his place? Would he see her again? Would his stuff be there? Had she used his shower? Touched her body with his soap?

By the time one a.m. hit, and he could clock out, he'd convinced himself she'd be gone, most likely with his cash stash. He probably should have been more discreet, but honestly, if she fled with it, then so be it. He kept the bulk of his savings in random spots—a chunk in the bank, more inside his mattress, a few wads tucked in the eaves of his old treehouse. Derek believed in being prepared. The jar held only his fun money.

He snoozed on the bus ride home. At his stop, he

hit the pizza place that stayed open late, picking up an extra-large loaded with meat. He'd skip the jog tonight in favor of push-ups and squats. Maybe watch the highlights of the hockey game.

To his surprise, Athena sat on his couch, wearing a soft pink sweater, his boxers, and a smile. "Do I smell pizza?"

"Yeah. Meat lovers, hope that's okay."

"Oh hell yeah." She vaulted off his sofa like a gymnast.

"Glad to hear it. So many folks going vegan these days. I tried it but didn't even last a week." He'd never been so damned hungry. Fucking tofu and veggies and fruits and nuts just weren't a meal to his carnivore brain.

"Fuck the rabbit food. Give me meat!" she declared, holding up a slice.

He'd love to give her his meat. Uh... He chewed, lest those words come out of his mouth.

As they ate, he asked her about her day. "So, did you have to escape any bad guys?"

She snorted. "Nope. Just dealt with my mom, did a bit of shopping, and then proceeded to suck searching stuff up on the internet."

His turn to make a noise. "That was your first mistake. Everyone knows the regular net only shows you what the government wants you to see."

A pizza slice hovered in the air in front of her mouth. "Hold on, are you a conspiracy theorist?"

"I'm sure some would call me that. I prefer the term well informed." He shrugged. "I don't take shit at face value. I like to hear both sides before I make an informed opinion."

"Fair enough. So how do you get your news?"

"Dark web," he stated before taking a bite of his pizza.

"Wait, that's a real thing?" Her eyes widened.

"Why would you think it wasn't?"

"Because I assumed it was like a thing they invented for movies." She waved a hand. "You know like for John Wick and the Marvels and stuff."

"It's real."

"And you can access it?" she asked, leaning forward, the vee of her sweater gaping. He averted his gaze but not before he got an eyeful of cleavage.

"Yeah. Just let me know what you want to find."

She chewed her lower lip. "That would mean involving you in my problem."

"And?"

"And these people I'm dealing with are kind of shitty."

"Obviously. All the more reason to let me help you."

"Let me think about it."

"You said you talked to your family?" he asked, changing the subject.

"Yeah. They're all right, if worried. Good thing our neighbor the psychic told her I was okay, or

Mom would have had the RCMP out searching for me."

"A psychic?" He laughed.

"You don't believe?"

"Nope."

"Says the guy with an apocalypse plan."

"Wait, how do you know I have one?" He frowned.

"Gun under the couch, crossbow under the bed, vacuum-sealed meal rations in the cupboard. Jugs of water in your linen closet."

She'd snooped, but he didn't take offense. He'd been known to do the same thing. Nothing like poking through some closets and cupboards to get a feel for a person. It kept him from getting involved with the chick who collected dolls. Dolls she later claimed killed a guy she was dating less than six months after Derek went to her place for dinner.

"The world is going to shit," he stated. "Figured it's best if I have some emergency supplies to tide me over just in case."

"You think it will be zombies or a nuclear blast?"

"I'm currently thinking alien invasion that triggers a nuclear blast, which then causes radioactive walking dead."

She didn't laugh at him. Not like some girls had. "With everything going on, you might be right. Let me guess, Grandma is just as prepared?"

"I'm small potatoes compared to her. She's got the

entire cellar under the house retrofitted as a bomb shelter. Air circulation, underground well, shelves and shelves of canned goods, rice, medicine." He spread his hands. "The plan is if the world gets fucked, I get my ass to her basement."

"Won't you be lonely?"

"She's got hundreds of movies, books, puzzles, games."

"Things to do, not people," she pointed out. "Unless you're planning to bang your grandma."

He wrinkled his nose. "No. But if I had a girlfriend, I'd be dragging her along."

"You're different from most guys," she murmured.

"Which probably explains why I'm single," he joked.

"I didn't mean it in a bad way. You're actually rather interesting."

"Why do I hear a but?"

"But you're too nice. You left me alone in your place after showing me your cash jar. Not too bright."

"It's just money." He rolled his shoulders. "And if you'd have taken it, then you obviously needed it."

"Too trusting by far." She cocked her head, and her lips curved slightly as she asked, "So what kind of partner are you in bed?"

He almost spat out the pizza crust in his mouth. He chugged some water before gasping, "What the fuck?"

"Don't be shy. I'm curious. You're obviously hot.

Despite your sometimes crude language, you're actually well-mannered. Kind. Funny. Not a pig. Your place is clean considering it's just you. You work. So you must have a flaw or someone would have snatched you up."

"Why would you assume I suck in the sack?"

"Do you?"

"No."

"How can you be sure?"

He gaped before mumbling, "Because I always make the woman come first."

"Doesn't make you good."

"I've never had complaints," he retorted. "What about you? Are you the kind who just likes to receive?"

"I don't lay there like a starfish, if that's what you mean."

"Any particular reason why we're even discussing sex?" Because he wasn't used to women being so bold. It was kind of a turn-on. Actually, everything about Athena revved his engine.

"I haven't fucked anyone in a while, and quite honestly, I miss it. Especially now that I'm kind of under a lot of stress."

"Is this your way of saying you want me to make you come?" he asked boldly because he got the impression she'd prefer him being direct.

"Yes. I would. That is, if you're in the mood."

"Am I alive?" he drawled. "Of course, I'm in the

mood, but don't you think it's kind of soon? We just met like a day ago."

"And? I'm not asking to marry you, just sex."

"Just sex," he repeated. "Okay. Let me know when."

"Now."

"Now?" The surprises kept on piling up.

"Unless you had other plans?" She arched a brow.

"No."

"Then no time like the present." She stood and, without preamble, stripped off her shirt.

He stared. Didn't blink. Didn't want to blink in case her breast-ly perfection disappeared.

"You going to get undressed?" she asked as she shoved at her pants.

"Shouldn't we, like, start by making out?" He'd never had a woman move so fast before.

"We'll kiss in a second. First, let's see what I've got to work with."

There was something a tad daunting about a woman standing there naked, hands on her hips, staring as he took off his work shirt. It wasn't boasting to admit he had a nice chest. He kept fit. His hands fumbled at his pants, though. Yeah, he knew his dick was above average at eight and a half inches, but would she like it and the slight tilt at the tip?

At least it didn't embarrass him by being limp. It sprang to attention the moment he freed it from his boxers.

Her lips curved. "That will do very nicely. Come here." She crooked a finger.

There wasn't a man alive who would have said no, and yet he hesitated. "Maybe we should hold off."

"Your dick says otherwise."

"You just came out of a traumatic situation."

She sighed. "Yeah, and I need relief. Something to remind me I'm alive. But I had to get stuck with the one guy with morals."

He shrugged. "Trust me, I'm not happy about it either."

"So what are we going to do if we don't fuck?"

"Hang out?"

"If we must," she stated dramatically.

He grinned as he dressed himself. He wanted to slap himself silly when she hid those gorgeous boobs, but at the same time, he wasn't one to take advantage.

She pursed her lips. "You know what, if you're not going to make me sing hallelujah, then maybe you can show off your dark web skills."

"My pleasure, but it does mean you'll have to tell me a bit more about what happened and what we're looking for."

"More like who." She paced his living room as he got out his laptop and set it up to crawl beyond the regular internet. Not something most knew how to do, but Derek had always had a curious nature. Combine that with his grandparents muttering about the evil government and he had a need to look beyond what the media liked to say.

"Where do you want me to start?"

She sat on the couch beside him, legs tucked up.

"The man I need to find is named Dr. Montgomery Rogers."

His fingers paused over the keyboard. "Wait, *the* Dr. Rogers? The guy who debunks myths?"

"Yeah."

"He kidnapped you?" His voice went a little high-pitched with incredulity.

"He did."

"But why?" he blurted out because it made no sense. Athena obviously wasn't a monster.

"Because the silly bastard seemed to think I was something I'm not." She laughed.

"Like what? An elf?" The first thing that came to mind because she had an ethereal beauty about her.

"Something like that," she murmured. She tilted her head and swept her hair. "No pointy ears, in case you were wondering."

"What exactly do you want to know about the doctor? Most of his work is public knowledge."

"Not really." She paused before adding, "He has a lab under one of the buildings at the Experimental Farm.

"Like fuck. Seriously?"

She nodded. "It's where I escaped from."

"Jeezus fucking Christ. That's insane." Also slightly unbelievable. Was she fucking with him?

"I know it sounds crazy, hence why I didn't want to tell you. Still having a hard time coming to grips with it myself, and yet I was there for almost a month."

"What happened while they held you captive?"

"Blood tests and other shit. Rogers kept trying to prove I had some weird genetic anomaly, which I don't."

"And now you want to find him? To do what?" He wasn't keen on being an accomplice to murder, especially of someone who would draw media attention. It was one thing when he thought they were dealing with a gang. No one gave a shit if they suddenly disappeared.

"I don't know. Maybe dig up some dirt to discredit him. Bring to light some of his unethical practices."

"You want to shut him down." That he could get behind. "Okay, let's see what we can find on this doctor."

Not much as it turned out. Despite the dark web being a bastion of information, there was a suspicious lack when it came to Montgomery Rogers, as if he didn't exist or someone had wiped his record clean.

"Well, this was a bust," Athena grumbled when he closed his laptop lid a while later.

"Yeah, it's weird. For a man that famous, there should have been something. I couldn't even locate a home address." Not to mention no connection to the

46

Experimental Farm in downtown Ottawa. Even his business had no office, just a postal box.

"Surveilling the farm will likely be noticed," she mused aloud as she rose to pace, her legs bare, given his boxers only went mid-thigh.

"Don't give up. Could be I'm not searching deep enough or he's mentioned but under an alias. We'll try again tomorrow. I gotta get to bed."

"Thank you," she murmured. "I really appreciate all you've done."

"No problem. You want the bed?"

"Depends. Will you be in it?"

He wanted to say yes. He shook his head. "We both know there wouldn't be any sleep happening, and I gotta work."

"Can't tempt you to play hooky?"

She sure could. At the same time, did he want to mess up his life for someone who would most likely disappear from it in a day or two? "You are tempting, but the bills need to be paid." He stood from the couch.

"In that case, good night." She leaned up on tiptoe to brush a kiss on his cheek and murmur, "Dream of me."

He did. And in the morning woke so hard he jerked off in the shower, a process that took an embarrassing thirty seconds. In the light of day, he couldn't believe he'd turned her down. He doubted he'd be so strong if she made the offer again.

She greeted him with a warm smile. "Morning, sugarplum."

"Hey, honey. You sleep okay?"

"Only after I played with myself, seeing as how someone left me hanging."

Yup, he spit out his coffee.

She laughed. "You're cute when you blush."

He did not blush. He did, however, mumble to escape, "I gotta get to work."

If he'd thought his last shift proved tediously long, this evening was even worse. To the point his supervisor pointed it out. "Not paying you to watch the clock."

Soon as Derek could leave, he booked it, actually making it home in under an hour, having caught all his buses. At times, he thought of getting a car, but the cost of parking it, plus insurance, and all the rest was a financial dent he couldn't justify. Usually, his commute didn't bother him. But that was before he had someone who excited waiting for him at home.

At least, he hoped Athena was still there. She'd said see you later when he left for work.

He walked in with some Chinese food he'd picked up to find her naked on his couch.

The bags almost hit the floor.

She turned a bright smile on him. "Honey, you're home."

Fuck yeah, he was. "I brought food."

"Ooh." She bounded over the couch, boobs bouncing, and he just about hit the floor in worship.

He tried to not focus on the hottie as he grabbed the plates and cutlery to eat.

"How was your shift?" she asked.

"Long," the honest truth. "What about you? Did you go out today?"

"For a bit. I put on a disguise and headed over to the Experimental Farm."

"Was that wise?" He spooned some rice onto his plate and dumped some crispy honey chicken on top.

"Probably not, but it didn't matter. Looks like the doctor cleared out."

"How can you tell?"

"Because Simon, the guard I flirted with, told me Rogers drives a Mercedes, and the parking lot most definitely didn't have one. It appeared rather empty."

"So what's next?"

She shrugged. "I don't know."

"Could be he isn't looking for you," he suggested.

"Is this your way of trying to kick me out?"

"No!" Almost shouted. "Stay as long as you'd like."

"Thanks, honey. Don't worry. I'll try to not cramp your style."

He almost said cramp it all you want. He'd not been this entertained in ever. However, there was something appetite-killing about sitting across from a woman eating. Not entirely correct. He might not be hungry for food, but damn, he craved something else.

And she knew it.

She tossed him a few coy looks before saying, "So am I masturbating for dessert, or are you going to cream me yourself?"

He'd been strong the night before.

He could not say no twice.

He rose from his side of the table, only to drop on his knees in front of her. Nothing was said. She just parted her legs and uttered a happy sigh as he leaned in for a lick of her pretty pink pussy.

She was wet. So very wet. And she moaned as he licked her. Moaned and grabbed hold of his hair as he spread her nether lips and teased her sex. He slid his hands under her ass, dragging her partially off the chair, changing the angle of her hips so he could thoroughly devour. Tasting her, teasing her. He flicked her clit with his tongue and was rewarded with a shudder.

He sucked her button while he thrust a finger into her.

She growled, "Give me another."

Two fingers thrust in and out as he plied her clit with attention. Her hands tugged at his hair. Her hips rolled and pushed against his mouth. The heels of her feet drummed his back.

Her channel tightened around his fingers, and her breathing emerged short and ragged. When she came, her pussy clenching and pulsing around his fingers, she wasn't quiet about it.

She yelled, "Oh fuck yeah," and he just about came in his pants.

Her eyes opened, and she gazed at him before purring, "Now that was what I call epic oral. Your turn next. Drop those pants, honey."

He couldn't stand and unbuckle his belt fast enough.

Just as her knees hit the floor and her hand gripped his straining dick, her head cocked as if she listened. He heard nothing, but she whispered, "I think we have company."

Not for long because his tight and very blue balls would kill them for interrupting.

CHAPTER 5

A QUITE TINGLY AND HAPPY ATHENA WAS also annoyed. After getting the most epic oral, she'd been excited to return the favor, but noises in the hall distracted. Especially since they seemed out of place at three a.m.

Poor Derek looked frustrated as he grumbled, "I don't hear anything."

Ah yes. His human ears wouldn't.

"Trust me when I say there's at least two people in the hall."

He didn't take her word for it and went to the apartment door to peek. He glanced at her and whispered, "Someone's put something over my peephole."

That someone probably listened too.

Rogers? Seemed most likely and unlikely all at once. No way could he have detected her already.

Athena dressed fast and padded to the door just as Derek yanked it open and barked, "What the fuck are you doing?"

Lo and behold, it was two of the thugs from the other night, still wearing their masks, but she recognized their scent.

And they'd come with a gun!

Not that Derek cared. "I fucking warned you pukes what would happen if I saw you again."

"We don't want you. Give us the girl."

"Nope." Derek blocked the doorway and crossed his arms.

"Are you blind?" said the smaller one. "We've got a gun."

"And no brains apparently," drawled her new lover.

"You either hand her over or I'll shoot!" The thicker fellow's hand had a slight tremble to it.

"Go ahead, and don't miss, because, this time, I won't be tossing you into a river," Derek snapped. "It's a long fall from the balcony."

Sweet, gentle, and kind unless you messed with him. Was there anything about this guy to hate?

"Just give us the girl and we won't put a hole in you," said the big guy.

"Yeah, no deal," Derek stated as he lunged. He grabbed the gun of the thicker fellow and yanked it free, which left him one-handed as the guy attacked. The other, knife in hand, wavered, probably not sure where to stab.

Athena slipped out and said, "Looking for me?" When the little guy turned his mask toward her, she punched him in the nose. When he didn't go down, she kneed him in the balls, and when he hunched over, she grabbed him by the head and gave him a knee to the face.

He hit the floor just as Derek knocked out the other guy. They eyed each other in the hall before both saying, "We should move them."

She giggled. "Jinx. Let's get them inside before your neighbors wake up and wonder what the hell."

He didn't ask why bring them in instead of tossing them out or calling the cops. She grabbed hold of the little guy and dragged him into the apartment while Derek handled the other.

Once in the apartment, she pursed her lips. "How long do you think they'll stay knocked out?"

"Might not be long so let's get them secured." Derek pulled some duct tape from a kitchen drawer. They each heaved their respective thug into a kitchen chair and wound the thick sticky fiber around them. Once done, they stood back and eyed them.

"So that's kind of fucked they came looking for you," Derek murmured.

"Apparently."

"Any idea why?"

"I can take a few guesses."

"Think they'll tell us who sent them?"

"With the right incentive they might."

"I ain't bribing them," he warned.

She snickered. "As if I'd want to reward them for being thugs."

"Nice jab by the way. Pretty sure I heard his nose crunch."

"My dad wanted us to know how to defend ourselves." Her dad would have liked Derek. They both believed in being prepared for the future.

"Remind me not to piss you off." He cupped his balls.

"Don't eat off my plate, always give me the bigger steak, and keep using that tongue like you just did and we'll get along fine, honey."

He laughed. "Deal, sugarplum."

In the midst of a messed-up situation, here they were, both smiling like loons.

"I'm going to wake up the big one," Derek stated.

"How?" she asked. "Don't tell me you have smelling salts."

"As if I'd waste any. Salt will be valuable if the world ends."

She didn't correct him on the difference in those salts. His apocalypse reply was cute.

He headed for the kitchen and ran the water before coming back with a bowl that he dumped on the head of the thick thug. The mask soaked up much of it, making the fabric hard to breathe through. The thug woke, choking and gasping. Only then did Derek pull off the mask.

The guy was young, maybe early twenties, with pockmarked skin, a tattoo of a cross over his left eye, and a bad attitude.

"Fucker," sputtered Tattoo.

"Says the guy who threatened me and my girl." Derek crouched and said softly, "I warned you to choose another path."

"We weren't coming after you. Just the woman."

"Why?"

"None of your fuck—"

Smack.

Derek casually smoked the guy before calmy asking again, "Why the fuck are you after my girl?"

She kind of liked the *my* part of that statement.

A sulking thug replied, "Because of the reward."

"What reward?" her sharp query.

The guy's gaze slewed to her, and he licked his lips. "The one posted to the message board."

Her brow creased. "What message board?"

The guy clammed up, but Derek had a reply.

"Judging by his tattoos, he's part of a gang. There's several of them now in town. I assume by message board he means something on the dark web."

"People post those kinds of things?"

Derek nodded. "It's quite common, actually." He eyed the thug. "What else did this post say?"

When the guy clammed his lips, Athena didn't have

to threaten, because Derek got in his face to softly say, "Answer the question."

"And if I don't?"

Derek swung and clocked the thug.

"What the fuck, man?"

"Here's the deal," Derek stated. "You came to my place looking to cause trouble. Kind of dumb. Especially since I warned you the last time that I never wanted to see your face again. So either you answer with your lips or my fists start talking to your face."

The thug sulked. "Ain't much to tell. Someone offered five grand for the woman. Posting had her face, said she might be using the name Athena."

"Shit," she muttered.

Derek glanced at her. "I take it this was a move by your previous acquaintances."

"Most likely. Five K, though? Kind of insulting."

His lips curved. "Agreed." His expression hardened as he turned to Tattoo. "Who posted it?"

"Dunno."

"Well, you must know something, else how are you supposed to collect?"

"The poster said if we found her to bring her to Bottoms Up and ask for Kyle."

"What's Bottom's Up?" she asked.

"A bar," Derek muttered. "A seedy one at that."

"Who did you tell I was staying here?" she questioned, wondering if they were already too late to flee.

EVE LANGLAIS

"No one," blustered Tattoo. "I wasn't sharing the prize. Just me and Ralph knew you was staying here."

"How did you know?" Derek snapped.

"Because we happened to see her out shopping and was following, but then she went into this building, and we didn't know what apartment. So we waited, and then we seen you," a comment directed at Derek. "And when you went inside, there was only one window that had light—"

"And you used your pea-sized brain to figure it out," she murmured. She felt dumb. Spotted by idiots and she'd not even noticed. She'd assumed her sensation of being watched was due to paranoia.

Derek had more questions. "Why did you assume she was with me?"

"Just a lucky guess." Tattoo tried to shrug, but the tape held him firm.

The smaller fellow woke and began thrashing and moaning. "Oh god, my face. My face. She broke my face."

"I'll rip out your tongue next if you don't shut it," Derek growled.

Sexy.

He removed Ralph's mask to show a kid barely out of his teens, also sporting the same tattoo over his eye. Derek shook his head. "Fucking idiots. Wasting your life and potential on cheap scores."

"Five grand is big bucks," argued Ralph.

"How much is your life worth?" Athena's sweet

58

reply. "Because here's the problem, boys. Now that you've seen me, I can't exactly let you go tattle."

Their mouths rounded. "We wouldn't tell," Tattoo hastened to state.

"Like I'm gonna believe you." Derek paced. "Where can we deposit their bodies? Canal won't spit them up for a few days or weeks, but carrying them that far will be a pain."

"We could dump them in the sewer," she suggested. "Keep them bound and the rats can have at them." She was only half serious, but curious where Derek went with this. She'd not gotten the impression he was a killer when he'd last confronted the thugs.

"The sewer is a good idea, but we'll have to tape their mouths shut, lest they whine too loudly and get discovered with all their parts intact."

"Dumpster fires are becoming more common," she stated. "Give them a joint or some smokes and the cops will assume they fell asleep with one lit."

"That's actually a good plan, but we'd have to remove the tape." Derek rubbed his chin. "Easy enough to knock them out so they stay put while they burn."

The thugs' eyes couldn't get any bigger or their fear-stink any worse.

"We won't tell," blubbered Ralph. "Promise."

"As if I'll believe a word out of your mouth," Derek snapped.

"Swear on my momma's life," sobbed the kid.

"And on my three babies," added Tattoo.

"Jeezus, you're a father?" Derek didn't hide his disgust. "Nice example you're setting."

"We'll leave you alone. We swear." The kid sounded sincere.

Would Derek actually kill them? Athena was tempted. These two were part of the problem Ottawa had with crime these days. Entitled, lazy assholes who thought they could take from those who worked hard.

"What do you think, sugarplum?" Derek asked her.

"I don't know, honey. The world might be better off without them."

"Please," sniveled Ralph. "I didn't even want to come. Horace made me do it."

"Did not," Horace exclaimed.

"Fuck you. You did. You knew I wanted to go straight, and when I said no, you said you'd tell Bethany I had crabs if I didn't."

As they argued, Athena sidled close to Derek to murmur, "Sorry I brought trouble to your doorstep."

"Don't you apologize."

"I will because this is my fault. I'll help you deal with these idiots then be on my way."

He whirled to glare. "No, you won't. We're sticking together."

"Why?"

He gave her a lopsided smile. "Because I do believe you're the chick I've been waiting for my whole life."

Well damn. Instant panty-wetter.

"You barely know me," she reminded.

"Grams always says your first impression of a person is usually right."

"Our first meeting you thought I was scamming you."

"Nah, my first thought was hubba-hubba."

She snorted. "And now?"

"Hubba-hubba, holy shit this chick is awesome."

She shook her head. "Definitely dropped on your noggin as a kid."

"Only a few times. Daddy says I was slipperier than a fat bass that doesn't want to be eaten."

She almost laughed and had to bite her lip.

Sudden silence had them both turning to eye the thugs who stared at them.

"Please don't kill me. I wanna do better," whispered Ralph.

"It's not me you've got to convince," Derek drawled. "So, sugarplum, what's the verdict? Kill them or set them free?"

"We can always kill them later," she suggested. "We're kind of tapped for time right now."

"I don't know. The chunky one looks like he's got loose lips."

"No, I don't." Horace pinched them tight.

"We've gotta go if we're gonna catch our flight," Derek stated. "I say we grab their wallets, take a pic of their ID's so we have their address. Then, if they blab, we'll know where to find them." Derek rummaged in their pockets and took images of their health cards and licenses.

Only then did he grab a knife, which had Ralph hyperventilating, even though Derek simply sliced through tape.

He stepped back and barked, "Git, and don't look back because if I ever see your faces again, I won't be so nice."

The thugs fled, and Athena sighed. "I'm really sorry about this."

"Why? This is the most interesting thing that's happened to me since Grandma sent me some homemade brownies."

"Must be good brownies."

"Not really, but the shrooms she adds to them give quite the trip."

Her mouth rounded before she laughed.

And laughed.

Then kissed him because, damn, she might be falling in love.

Alas, the kiss went nowhere, as Derek set her apart and sternly stated, "No distracting me. We've got to get moving."

"Why? You think they'll rat us out?"

"Maybe. But I'm more concerned about the fact whoever is looking for you put out a reward. Who knows how many folks have seen you? If dumb and dumber can track you down, then I'm worried someone with a little more smarts might, too."

"Where can we go?"

His eyes danced with mirth as he said, "Wanna meet my grams?"

CHAPTER 6

DEREK DIDN'T HAVE A CAR, NOR DID HE WANT to waste the funds renting one. So he did what he always did when he wanted to visit his grandparents.

Called.

"What do you fucking want?" barked his grams.

"Hey, you old bat, you still kicking?" he asked. He sat in a coffee shop a few blocks from his place with a disguised Athena sitting across from him, putting back eggs, bacon, sausage, and toast like she'd not just devoured a full meal just over an hour ago. A duffel bag at his feet held his personal effects. AKA his Xbox and anything with his name on it plus the few items Athena had picked up.

"You ain't inheriting yet, you mooching bastard," Grams' retort.

"Inherit what? Your ugly-ass couch and granny panties?"

"You wish. I'm leaving you the dust bunnies under my bed, you ungrateful turd."

Derek laughed, even as he saw a listening Athena frowning at him over a forkful of eggs. "Love you too, Grams."

"Why you calling so early? You finally break a few laws and need us to bail you out of the clink?"

"Alas, I'm still a good boy. However, I do need a place to crash for a few."

"You in trouble?" Grandma asked.

"Not exactly, but the friend I'm helping is. She'll be with me."

A pause. "I don't like strangers."

"Are you sure you won't make an exception for my girlfriend?" he stated, despite it not being exactly true. He could have told Grams the truth—hey, I met this chick who's really hot and has some bad shits after her. Grandma would have welcomed Athena with open arms, as she loved drama even as she claimed she didn't.

But saying the G word? That would really put his grams in a tizzy.

"Who the fuck is dumb enough to date you?"

He grinned. "Guess you'll soon find out."

"I take it you're calling for a ride?"

"Yeah."

Rather than go on a rant about how he should own a car, she muttered, "Meet Gramps at the usual place in forty-five minutes."

"Thanks."

"Whatever." Her way of saying I love you.

He hung up, and Athena eyed him over her glass of orange juice. "You weren't kidding about your grandma."

"You heard?"

"Kind of hard not to. What was it like growing up being called a bastard?"

"No worse than the kid being called champ or pumpkin. I always knew she loved me, and words are just that. It's the intent that counts."

"Sticks and stones," she murmured in reply.

"Exactly, so keep that in mind when she decides on your nickname."

Her brow arched. "You mean I'll get one of my own?"

"Oh, hell yeah."

"What did she call your last girlfriend?"

"Nothing since she never met her. The last one I brought around was like five years ago. Cindy Brown. Grandma took one look at her and called her the harpy on account Cindy had a thing for telling me, and others, what to do."

"I'm surprised you'd date someone like that since you seem to have a mind of your own."

"In my defense, she had a great rack."

She blinked.

He coughed. "Yours is better."

"Have you ever been serious with someone?"

"Yeah. My last girlfriend, who kept finding excuses

to not meet my grandma. Should have been my first warning. When I suggested we move in together because she kept bitching she never saw me, she went a little psycho and accused me of stifling her."

"I hate it when people play dumb games like that."

"Me too," he retorted. "Like, why is it so hard to be honest and real?"

"You're an interesting man," she lightly stated.

"Says the queen of mystery. Come on, we've got a bit of a walk to meet Gramps."

"Why doesn't he grab you at your place?" she asked as he dropped cash on the table and they left the diner, the duffel bag slung on his back.

"Because I'm technically not supposed to be living there. I'm subletting from a guy who's out of the country but not via legal channels. He needs an address to make it seem like he's there but didn't want to leave the place vacant. So I rent it for cheap and have all my mail sent to my grandparents' place."

"That doesn't explain why you get picked up away from your building."

"Because Grandma is convinced the feds are watching them and doesn't want to lead them to my apartment."

"And why are the feds watching her?"

"Because of the pot and shrooms she grows."

"Pot is legal now."

"Now, yes, but it didn't used to be, and old habits die hard." He glanced at her, and to his surprise, she didn't laugh or act shocked. Most women took issue with the family business. A business he wasn't involved in, but still, folks heard the words "marijuana crop" and got weird.

"I'm assuming, with the pot and fed thing, your grandma's got security at her place?"

"Yup. Cameras, dogs, traps—"

"Traps?"

"Yeah, I wouldn't recommend wandering through the woods alone. I know what to watch for, but it can be dangerous for the unknowing. Pits, snares, trip lines, just to name a few. If someone did manage to follow, they'll be in for a surprise."

"Seems unlikely since you're not legally registered to that apartment. Means even if dumb and dumber talk, they won't be able to trace you."

"Unless they break in and go through my stuff and find something I forgot."

Her lips pursed. "Hopefully that doesn't happen."

"Even if they do figure out we went to the farm, they'll have a hard time because Grams don't like strangers."

"Maybe I shouldn't go. I wouldn't want to bring trouble to them."

He snorted. "Don't say that to Grams. She'd be insulted."

"We should warn her, though."

"I was planning to. She's always looking for a reason to buy more guns."

She blinked. "How many does she own?"

"Let's just say she could outfit a militia."

Athena shook her head. "I feel like I'm in the Twilight Zone."

"I promise she and Gramps are good people despite some of their beliefs."

"Oh, I believe you. My family is different than most as well. We just don't collect weapons or set booby traps." Her lips twitched. "Although I'll bet Ares would be interested."

"Older or younger brother?" he asked.

"Middle child. Selene is the baby."

"Must have been cool having siblings growing up."

"Sometimes. Other times we were screaming and yelling and fighting. Dad used to let us go at it, but Mom had this thing about us talking it out, hugging, and apologizing."

"Which was better?" he asked.

"Honestly, when Ares tore the head off my favorite Barbie, I took great pleasure in hiding his video games and making him beg for their return."

"I sometimes wished I had siblings growing up, but when Mom left, Dad wasn't interested in dating. Still isn't. My mother broke him."

"And my mom never recovered from my father dying." She paused before adding, "I think the hardest part was his death was preventable. He was shot while hiking in the forest."

"Jeezus, that's fucking shit," he exclaimed. "Sorry, I mean that sucks."

"Yeah, it does. For a while, she wouldn't let us leave the yard she was so terrified we'd be taken from her too."

He spotted the gas station up ahead. "Almost there. Gramps should be along any minute."

Athena cocked her head as if listening, and yet once more he heard nothing. "What is it?"

"Sounds like someone lost their muffler."

Her hearing must be good. "That's Gramps. He drives an old Ford and does most of the repairs himself. He's patched the exhaust system I don't know how many times, but he won't replace the baffles. Says a truck should growl."

"I'm surprised the cops haven't given him a ticket."

"They have, but he's got a friend who's good at making them go away."

"Useful."

He pointed. "There he is."

The forest-green truck, with a white stripe down each side, rumbled into view. Gramps pulled up alongside them, and Derek opened the passenger door.

"Hey, Gramps. Thanks for the ride. Sorry for the early wakeup call."

The old man, fit for his age, if thick, grunted. "I was already up. I was about to hit the blind when you called."

Derek glanced at Athena. "Hunting blind. Deer season just opened."

"Your grandma has said I better snag at least three since the price of beef went up again. Let's go. I should still have time to hike it before dawn."

While Derek stood, ready to boost Athena into the truck, she required no aid, swinging herself into the cab and scooching over the bench seat that spanned the front. Derek clambered in and no sooner shut the door than Gramps was speeding away but not before saying, "Don't know what you're thinking bringing this sweet thing to see your grams. She's gonna eat her alive."

To which Athena replied, "I can't wait."

Neither could Derek, because he might have finally met the one woman who could hold her own with his family.

CHAPTER 7

ATHENA WONDERED WHY SHE'D LET DEREK talk her into going to his grandparents'. The right thing to do when those thugs showed up looking for her would have been to hightail it. She could have asked to borrow some more cash and taken off into the great big unknown.

Instead, she was squished between two large men, on her way to a booby-trapped farm with an outspoken old lady.

Admittedly, despite her trepidation involving them, she was kind of excited. Derek kept fascinating her, from his great attitude to his sense of humor. And that body... Damn that body was hot, and his tongue even better. She couldn't wait for some alone time to finish what they began.

But first, time to play nice with grandpa.

"So you got a name?" the grandpa asked.

"Athena. And you are?"

"The young'uns all call me Gramps. Where you from?"

"Calabogie area. My mom has a farm."

"You don't say. Ours is down in the Richmond area. Wonder if we know your place."

"You might. Beatrice's Honey Bee Emporium?"

"No shit." Gramps took his eyes from the road for a second. "Grams swears by your shit. Says you can tell they pay attention to the flowers they're letting the bees feed on."

"Mom takes her flavors very seriously." Athena paused before saying, "I hear you grow weed and mushrooms."

Gramps snorted. "Yup. We do. Surprised the boy told you."

She glanced at Derek. "He's pretty honest. One of the things I like about him."

"He'd better not be a liar, or the belt will be kissing his ass." A growled threat.

Derek didn't cringe, but he did laugh. "You still got that thing?" He nudged Athena. "I was raised with the spare the rod, spoil the child mantra."

"Did you get whooped often?"

"Not too much, but enough. I could be a little shit."

"Little? Your grams still hasn't forgiven you for using her fine China for target practice."

"In my defense, she never used them, complained

they needed constant dusting, and they exploded really cool when shot."

Grandpa snorted. "Never said you didn't do us a favor."

"How long have you and your wife been married?" Athena asked.

"Coming up on fifty-five years. We married young. Eighteen years old."

"High school sweethearts?" she queried.

"Of sorts. I accidentally knocked her up and had to make an honest woman out of her."

"Grams says you did it on purpose," Derek interjected.

"And if I did? She was the hottest girl in school. Smart too. Too smart for a dumb farmer like me, so I put a bun in her oven to make her mine."

Athena's mouth rounded. "You intentionally impregnated her?"

"Yup." Gramps sounded proud. "Best thing I ever did."

"Does she agree?"

"I'm still alive, ain't I?"

Derek muttered, "It's a wonder given how much you smoke."

"Bah. I'm more likely to croak if I stop at this point." Gramps skewed a gaze at her. "So, what you do for a living?"

"I was a lab technician."

"Was? Did you quit? Kids nowadays, never sticking to stuff," grumbled Gramps.

"More like fired since I stopped showing up. Not on purpose, I should add. I ran into some trouble."

"What kind of trouble?"

She eyed Derek, who murmured, "Up to you what you want to divulge, but you should know Gramps is cool."

She hesitated before murmuring, "Kidnapped and held hostage by a doctor who thought I had interesting genetics for his experiments."

Gramps stiffened beside her. "Wait, you're hiding from a doctor?"

"Yeah."

"Did you report him and have him arrested?"

"If only it were that simple," she muttered. "Let's just say he's got friends in high places. It wouldn't go well for me if I came forward."

"Bloody quacks with their pills. Don't you worry, little sweetie. If that doc comes sniffing around the farm, we'll make him wish he'd become a car salesman," Gramps declared.

Derek leaned close to whisper, "One down. One to go."

Wait, did that mean his grandpa liked her?

The ride didn't take long, and soon they were pulling into a long drive. Very long. Lined with trees, the asphalt only wide enough for one vehicle. The rising sun bathed the forest and then the fields that followed with warm rays. The crops had all been mown and the ground churned, ready for winter. She saw some goats grazing and pointed.

"I didn't know you had animals."

"We have a couple. A few goats for weed control and poison ivy. Chickens for eggs and meat. Two pigs, a handful of cows, some horses, a few dogs, some barn cats—"

She interrupted. "That's more than a couple."

He grinned. "Maybe more accurate to say a couple of each."

"Any problems with wildlife? Coyotes? Wolves?" She threw that in casually, wondering if another lycanthrope had a claim on this area.

"Wolves don't stray this close to the city. As for coyotes..." Gramps chuckled. "You should see the carpet I made from their fur in my den."

They pulled up in front of a large farmhouse. Painted white clapboard siding. The roof gray metal. The shutters a dark blue that matched the front door. A hound lay on the porch and didn't move as Derek jumped out of the truck, but it lifted its head and growled when Athena appeared.

"Don't you be nasty to our guest, Rosy," Gramps hollered.

Not Rosy's fault. She smelled the predator in Athena. But Athena knew how to deal with canines. She approached the dog and crouched, crooning, "Hey, Rosy. Who's a good guard dog?" Sweet words, soft tone, but she fixed an intense stare on the dog and bared her teeth slightly.

Rosy didn't argue about who was boss but did duck her head before inching forward for pets.

The door swung open, and a woman boomed, "Where's the little bastard and his hussy?" With snowy-white hair and a thick frame that matched the big voice and personality, it could only be Grams.

"Right here, you old bat." Derek dragged his grandma into a hug that lifted her off the ground and growled, "Be nice to Athena."

"Why? Is she a pussy who can't handle conversation?" snapped Grams as he set her on her feet.

Athena held out her hand. "Nice to meet you, ma'am. Thanks for your hospitality."

"Don't thank me yet. Did the bastard warn you that everyone staying here is expected to chip in and help?"

"I'd be delighted. I've not seen my family farm in months, so it will be nice to get my hands dirty again."

"Your family has a farm?" Grams asked suspiciously.

"Her mom runs that honey place you like," Gramps stated, stomping up the porch steps, cigarette dangling from his lips.

"Really?" Grams eyed her up and down. "You don't look like your ma."

"I take after my dad's side."

"Like the little bastard. Poor fucker. He wasn't blessed. Not one bit." Grams shook her head.

Derek didn't take offense but grinned. "I might be hideous, but at least I've got Gramps' good hair and my grams' shining personality."

Grams snorted. "Such an ass. Get inside. I've got breakfast just about ready. You hungry?"

"Very," Athena exclaimed. She didn't shy away from food. Shifting burned a lot of calories.

"You one of them vegan, meat-hating bitches common in the city?" Grams asked as she led the way inside.

"Hell no. If given the choice between eating only veggies the rest of my life or meat, I'd choose meat."

"What if the apocalypse wipes out all animals?" Grams queried as she entered a massive kitchen with huge wooden cabinets and a butcher-block-topped island.

"I'd eat people. After all, meat is meat."

Grams paused by the counter to stare at her but directed her question at Derek. "Where did you find this girl?"

"Naked by the canal."

"Turning tricks?"

Athena coughed. "More like escaping some assholes who thought it was okay to kidnap me."

"You got away?" At Athena's nod, Grams added, "Did you pay them back?"

"Not yet. But don't worry, they won't get away with what they did."

Grams offered a feral grin. "Let me know if you need a gun or a grenade. I have a rocket launcher, too, but those tend to draw attention. How do you like your eggs?"

"On a plate," she replied.

"Sit your ass down. I'll have them ready in a minute."

Athena slid into a kitchen chair, with Derek sitting beside her. Gramps took the head of the table, and despite the sound of eggs sizzling, Grams whipped him up a coffee and placed it in his hand. Strange given the woman's outspoken nature.

Seeing her surprise, Derek leaned close to whisper, "Grams has some old-school ideas, feeding her man being one of them."

Indeed, Gramps got the first plate, then Derek, Athena next, and then Grams herself.

It was heaven. Fat sausages drizzled in maple syrup, crispy bacon, potato hash, and toasted bread she had the feeling wasn't store-bought. The orange juice tasted fresh squeezed. She cleared her plate using a fourth piece of toast to sop up the runny yolk of her over-easy egg.

By the time she finished, she caught Grams watching her. "You eat good," she remarked.

"Blame the cook. That was delicious." Athena then rose, grabbed her plate, and stacked it onto

Derek's. Then she went to grab Gramps', but Grams already had it.

"I'm off to get you a buck," announced Gramps.

"Take the boy with you so you don't throw out your back again."

Derek glanced at Athena, a question in his eyes. She gave him a slight nod. "Make it a fat one. I love venison steak."

As the men left, Athena stood at the sink and began washing. Grams started drying quietly before saying, "Who's chasing you?"

"A doctor."

"Why would a doctor be so interested in a girl?"

"Good genetics?"

"Bullshit."

She shrugged. "I know it sounds nuts, but he really was interested in my DNA. He took lots of blood and samples."

"Looking for what?"

"You'd have to ask him." Athena rinsed a plate and put it on the rack before adding, "There's a chance he'll track me here."

"Ain't worried about a doctor."

"He won't come alone, and the people he brings will most likely be armed."

Grams chuckled. "So am I."

"I don't want to see anyone hurt because of me."

"Yet here you are."

"Because Derek kind of made me."

Grams snorted. "I doubt anyone can make you do shit."

"Fine, I'll admit I was curious. He talks about you a lot."

"Of course, he does, we're his family."

They finished the dishes, and Athena rinsed out the sink before asking, "What can I do to help?"

"You afraid of messing up your nails?" Grams had a sly expression that probably didn't bode well, but Athena accepted the challenge.

"What do you need?"

Apparently, Athena needed to pass some kind of test, which was why Derek found her mucking out the pig pen.

CHAPTER 8

"Fuck me. Why didn't you tell Grams to fuck off?" Derek exclaimed when he saw his pretty Athena sweaty from shoveling shit. He knew Grams was behind it because no one ever volunteered to do it. Pig shit stank.

"Bah. It's just poop. No biggie," Athena huffed as she finished the last of the shoveling and began laying fresh hay on the dirt.

"It's usually my job, and she knew I would get to it once I finished helping Gramps hang the buck," he growled.

"Then I guess I saved you some work." She climbed over the fence to stand by him. "You seem to forget I'm not some fragile damsel incapable of work. I was raised on a farm, remember?"

"You're a guest."

"Who might be bringing trouble to your family's doorstep. Least I can do is be useful."

"You're being too nice." His dark expression didn't detract from his handsomeness. Although she did prefer his smiles.

"I don't mind. After being cooped up for a month, it's nice to get some real exercise."

"I can't believe they had you for that long." What he wouldn't do to get his hands on the sick fucks who took her.

"It took me a bit before I figured out a way to escape."

"How did you get out?"

"Pretended I was going to bang a guard. Stole his access codes instead and bolted."

A pretend seduction explained why she was naked when they met. "Glad you found a way."

"So what's next on the chore list?"

"You can sit your ass down while I handle the chimney. It needs some bricks reset, and Grams doesn't want Gramps up on the ladder."

"I'll give you a hand."

"You good with heights?"

"I'm good at all kinds of things," she purred.

Instant erection. He still remembered the taste of her and wanted nothing more than to get back between those thighs. "Wouldn't mind a spotter. We'll grab the stuff from the shed then go at it."

As they walked across the yard, she queried, "Aren't you tired? You never got to sleep after your work shift."

"I got a bit of a nap in the bus and in the blind while Gramps watched. I'm also used to working odd hours. Sometimes, I'll be just getting home when I get a call about a fire. So long as I'm moving, I'll be fine. But the moment I sit my ass in a comfy chair, expect snoring."

"I can fix the bricks if you need a snooze."

"And have Grams give me hell for letting my girlfriend do my task? Oh, hell no."

"Girlfriend?"

The word had slipped out, so he offered a cover. "Calling you my girlfriend might keep Grams from going too hard at you."

"Seems to me she'll be more likely to test my limits to make sure I'm good enough for you."

Astute observation. "As my girlfriend, we can share a bed." A casual statement.

"I thought you wanted to sleep," she chirped.

He stumbled. "Maybe I will sneak another nap later, in that case."

She laughed. "You'd better be ready to go because we have some unfinished business."

Hell yeah, they did, and he couldn't wait.

As they worked on the chimney, then some fencing that needed new wire, Derek found himself watching Athena. How the tip of her tongue peeked when she concentrated. How she casually pulled back her long hair and twisted it into a knot to keep it out of her face. How she had this habit of turning her head left and right and sniffing. She scented almost as much as the dog did.

Her free spirit had him laughing a few times, especially when they took a break and she spotted a rabbit and took off after it, legs pumping as if she fully intended to catch it barehanded.

Later that afternoon, with their chores done, he took her down to the creek. This time of year it wasn't too deep or fast flowing. Spring, though, watch out.

He stripped his shirt at the edge and tossed it onto a flat rock. His hands went to his pants next.

"Skinny-dipping?" she asked, once more doing that short inhalation thing as if she tested the air.

"Nothing like it after a day's work." He stepped out of his jeans.

"I haven't done that since I was a teen," she admitted before joining him in the buff. No qualms about stripping at all. He kind of loved that about her.

No way he could hide his hard-on, and she licked her lips as she eyed him.

He wagged a finger. "Not right now. I'm not into getting grass stains on my knees."

"There's other ways of doing it that don't involve lying down."

Jeezus, she knew exactly what to say.

He waded into the creek, knowing where it dropped so that he could submerge.

She joined him, laughing as she said, "It's cold!"

"Refreshing," he countered.

She joined him, slippery and wet, lacing her arms around his neck and planting a kiss on him. "Thanks."

"For what?"

"For everything."

"Bah." He wasn't about to be thanked for doing the right thing. Especially since he seemed to be benefitting the most. Spending time with Athena was bringing him more pleasure than he could have imagined.

Until she dunked him.

He came up sputtering. "Now you're in for it!" he declared.

They splashed in the water, dunking, chasing, with lots of touching that left a lingering tingle. Abruptly, she ceased playing and cocked her head.

"Someone's coming."

Once more, she heard things he couldn't and was on the shore in a flash, her bare ass lightly jiggling as she ran not for the pile of clothes but for the woods. He heard a yell, a male one, and he couldn't move fast enough, dick and balls swinging, to reach Athena.

He found her atop a man, her knee digging into his chest, her face low as she growled, "Who sent you?"

"No one, ma'am," the fellow on the ground, wide-eyed with shock, exclaimed.

"Liar. Don't make me hurt you."

While amused, Derek came to the rescue. "He's not lying, sugarplum. That's my second cousin, Frank."

And his arrival didn't bode well because where Frank went, trouble inevitably followed.

CHAPTER 9

ATHENA SLOWLY ROSE FROM THE MAN SHE'D pinned to the ground. His gaze followed, lingering on her girly bits, and Derek noticed. He shifted his position to block her from view before snapping, "What the fuck, Frank?"

"Sorry, coz. Grams sent me out to find you. Something about Gramps needing a hand checking Conan's shoe."

"Fine. Message delivered. Tell them I'll be along in a few."

Dismissed but Frank didn't leave. He rose from the ground and held out his hand. "We haven't been properly introduced. I'm Frank Kennedy. And you are?"

Before Athena could reply, Derrick growled, "My girlfriend so you can stop leering."

The claim arched Frank's brows. "Didn't know you were dating."

"Probably 'cause it ain't your business." Derek's tone remained low and hard, making it obvious there was no love lost between them.

"Chill, coz. Didn't mean to piss you off. I'll head back to the house. See you later."

Frank wandered away, and Athena couldn't help her amusement as she said, "You're cute when you're jealous."

"I'm not jealous," Derek grumbled as he headed back for the creek's edge and their clothes.

"Then what was that display?"

"Frank is a troublemaker."

"In what way?" she asked as she tugged on her clothes.

"Always getting into scrapes and claiming innocence. Shoplifting and claiming he had no idea he'd put the stuff in his pocket. Gambling. Trying to get my grandparents to invest in sketchy deals."

"They seem too smart to fall for that."

"They are, but that doesn't stop Frank from trying. Last year he tried to convince them to sell the farm. Even brought by a buyer. I thought Grams was going to kill him."

"I'm surprised she allows him to set foot on the property."

"She tried to ban him, but Gramps feels sorry for Frank on account he lost his parents in a car crash. Says they're the only family Frank's got. Fucker could disappear and I'd be fine with it, though." Such intense dislike.

"Which of your girlfriends did he make a pass at?" A wild guess but call it a feeling.

"All of them. As a teen, he used to spend the summers here because his parents would go off to some foreign place as volunteers. He made moves on every single girl I was interested in."

"I hope they slapped him."

"No." His glum reply. "Frank has a way about him that women like. Not to mention the looks."

"You're better looking," she stated. And it was the truth. There was something a little too slick and cocky about Frank. The type of guy who thought he was god's gift to women. The type she liked to slap.

"You're just saying that because I made you come," he replied lightly.

"That's just a bonus. Handsome *and* orally talented."

"You don't have to stroke my ego."

She stood in front of Derek to stop him in his tracks then looked him in the eye as she placed a hand over his package and murmured, "I will stroke it if I want, and you will love it."

He went a tad cross-eyed before dragging her close for a kiss and a whispered, "Fuck me, you're amazing."

"Yes, I am. And don't you forget it."

How surreal. In captivity a few days ago and now

flirting with a guy she really liked. Would this go anywhere? Usually, she'd say no. She didn't do relationships because most guys annoyed her pretty quick. But thus far, Derek only intrigued her more and more.

Her sister would be laughing her ass off to see her smitten. While Selene was a big believer in romance and love, Athena had never been afflicted.

Until now.

They reached the house, and Derek sent her upstairs to shower and change first due to the single bathroom. She'd tried to convince him to join her, but he shook his head. "While I'd like to, can you imagine Grams' reaction?"

The old lady would probably have plenty to say, but it would have been worth it.

Athena showered quickly and changed into ill-fitting jeans—the shape of them conformed to their last owner before getting thrifted—and a hoodie that stated, Class of 2017. She really would need to do something about her wardrobe.

She headed downstairs to find Derek glowering in the kitchen, while Frank, perched on a stool, regaled Grams cooking at the stove.

"...and I told the guy, no way am I paying that much for a fake. And he then says, well how much would you pay?"

Derek saw her enter and rolled his eyes. She grinned and then, because Frank had paused to watch her, strolled to Derek and planted a kiss on his lips. "Shower's all yours, honey."

"I'll have one later."

Grams whirled from the stove, wooden spoon in hand. "You'll go now, smelly bastard."

"Guess that dip in the creek left you dirtier than expected," Frank taunted.

"I wouldn't say that," Athena quipped. "I'm feeling very refreshed. It's very good for easing tension." While they'd not gotten to the climax part, they would have if not interrupted. And honestly, playing as they had did much to relax her.

Frank gaped, and Derek did his best to not laugh, but she noticed the smolder in his eyes. Most likely he remembered her promise for tonight.

Derek stood. "I'll be back in a few." He glanced at Frank. "Try to not be a dick."

"Who me?" Frank clutched his chest.

"Feel free to slap him for me," Derek told Athena as he left.

"Come and tell me about yourself." Frank patted the seat beside him. Athena joined him at the island but kept a stool empty between them. While she had no interest in the guy, she didn't want Derek thinking she might. Not given their history.

"So what do you work as?" she asked, gladly taking the fresh slice of bread Grams slid to her on a plate, already buttered. And hot. Oh my god, it was freshly baked. Happily chewing, Athena barely paid any attention to Frank.

"Currently, I'm between projects."

"Unemployed. How surprising," she drawled.

He frowned, sensing the jab but not sure how to respond. "I like to change things up. Don't want to get bored. What about you?"

"I'm a lab technician."

"I would have pegged you for a model," he stated with a smile.

"Oh hell no. I'd rather do something that doesn't rely on being objectified," she exclaimed.

"You sure?" Frank insisted. "I've got some contacts who could take some test shots and get them to the right people."

"Who would then claim I needed to blow or bang someone for a job. No thanks."

"What?" Frank gasped.

"I know how show biz works, and I'm not interested in getting on my knees to make a buck."

Grams remained quiet. A surprise.

Frank no longer had the smarmy smirk. "Well excuse me for trying to help."

Playing the victim. How predictable. Athena cocked her head. "So how many baby mommas do you have? Given your age, late thirties, I'll say at least three."

"I'm only thirty-one!" he sputtered.

"You didn't answer the question."

Frank glared, and Grams turned to reply. "He's at four and still won't get it snipped."

Athena tsked. "Some men are so irresponsible."

"Accidents happen," Frank whined.

"Four times?" Athena snorted. "You're nothing like Derek."

"Thank God," Frank muttered.

"Yeah, because why would you want to be good-looking, decent, and funny?"

"Derek's not funny!" huffed the annoying cousin.

"Then you must lack a sense of humor." She then ignored Frank to address Grams. "I'm sorry. How rude of me to just sit here eating your delicious bread. How can I help with dinner?"

For a second, Grams appeared ready to refuse her offer then pointed. "Cutlery is in the drawer. Glasses and plates above it in the cupboard."

Athena set the table, ignoring the sulking Frank, which was how Derek found them, hair wet and slick, his skin still dewy from his shower. He eyed her and appeared surprised.

What, did he not think her capable of basic manners? Momma would have kicked her ass if she caught Athena being a rude guest.

Dinner proved interesting. Grams mostly spoke to Athena and Derek. Gramps shoveled food. Frank kept trying to dominate the conversation, but Athena more or less ignored him.

The apple pie for dessert filled her belly nicely,

and when Grams shooed her and Derek to the porch, refusing her offer to help with dishes, Athena leaned against him in the two-seater swing.

"Your grandparents are nice," she murmured.

"Only because they like you."

"How can you tell?" she asked.

"Because Grams never lets anyone help her in the kitchen."

Which explained his expression when he caught her setting the table.

"Your cousin, though, is an ass."

"Told you," he chirped.

"I can't believe anyone in their right mind would choose him over you."

"Guess they weren't as smart as my sugarplum," he teased.

"Blind, too. You're way hotter."

"Let's go to bed," he suddenly said.

"I thought you'd never ask."

They headed up to his room, the queen-sized bed big enough for two. But they didn't fuck. Fatigue, along with a food coma set in, and Athena found herself being cuddled.

Yes, spooned by a man, and she didn't mind it one bit.

Although she could have killed the rooster that woke her at the crack of dawn.

But then forgave it when Derek began kissing her

neck. She rolled over in the bed and reached beneath the covers to grip him.

"I wouldn't if I were you."

"Afraid you'll blow."

"Yesss," he hissed.

She kept stroking, and he growled, "Brat. Now be quiet."

Athena was about to ask why when he disappeared under the blanket.

"My turn again?" she whispered.

Rather than reply, he positioned himself between her thighs. At the first lick of his tongue across her pussy, she shoved a fist in her mouth. Even then, she made noise. How could she not when he pleasured her, spreading her lips to lap and tease? He delved with his tongue then flicked her clit. When her hips started rocking, he pinched it with his lips and almost got knocked out as she bucked.

She managed to gasp, "I want you in me before I come."

"Hold on, need a condom." He grabbed one from the nightstand and had it on in seconds.

He crawled up her body until his lips met hers. As they kissed, his hard cock pressed against her pussy.

She wiggled until the head went where she wanted it.

Inside her.

He buried his face against her shoulder as he thrust, his breathing as erratic as hers as he pumped, his thick shaft filling her nicely. The curve at the tip? Pure delight as it butted against her G-spot.

He pistoned in and out, the strokes deep and hard, and she clung to him. Clung to him as he rode her. Clung to his cock as he slammed it in and out.

When she came, his lips were there to catch her strangled cry.

He held her after, rolling so she lay atop him, his hand lazily stroking her back until she sighed.

It led to Derek murmuring, "Now that's what I call a good start to the morning."

A good start to the day.

Which turned into a week.

Derek took a leave of absence from his work. Together, they helped around the farm, the familiar tasks soothing.

On the second week, she got a message to her new online account that indicated her mom and siblings had returned home. Ares had been watching the farm and said the coast appeared clear. Perhaps Rogers had given up. Caught up in Derek, she'd certainly put her plot for revenge on a backburner. In a sense, she should thank Rogers. He'd been instrumental in the events that led to her meeting Derek.

By the third week, she'd settled into a routine with Derek and his grandparents. One big happy family—minus the cousin who left the day after he'd visited. Grams had even taken her to town to get some clothing that wasn't hideous, stating she'd more than earned them with her work.

As they entered week four, and with the full moon pending, reality set in.

How would she hide the coming change from Derek? They spent most of their time together. They slept together each night. He'd notice if she slipped away.

While it killed her a bit inside, she had to lie. "I need to go away for a day," she told him as they lay snuggled in bed.

"Why?" he asked, stroking her arm as he spooned her.

"Family stuff. It will just be for one night."

"Want me to come along?"

"No. It's kind of personal."

He stiffened. Most likely insulted.

What excuse could she use to fix this? "It's to do with my sister. Girly business."

He relaxed. "Can I at least give you a ride?"

She allowed it, letting him drop her in Calabogie at the Redneck Bistro. She waved as he left.

And really hoped that wasn't the last time she'd see him.

CHAPTER 10

ATHENA NOT WANTING DEREK AROUND WHILE she met her sister bothered. This last month had been incredible. In Athena, he'd found someone who engaged him in every respect. It wasn't just the great sex. It was the way they talked and joked, her work ethic, the way she got along with his grandparents. Even his dad had been by the farm a few times and declared to Derek in private, *"She's a keeper."*

He agreed but for one thing.

Athena had a secret, and he got the feeling it involved the reason why she'd been kidnapped and held prisoner, an event she still wouldn't discuss in detail. He'd tried prodding, and outright asking, but she lied and said she didn't know why they'd picked her. *"Guess I fit a profile,"* was her reply.

But he had to wonder. Could it be because of her insanely good hearing? She'd gone hunting with him and always knew well before him when a turkey or buck headed for the blind.

Her sense of smell? More than once she'd guided him to a spot she said felt lucky. Each time, whatever they were seeking—grouse for cooking, coyotes bugging the hens, a lost goat—she unerringly seemed to find them.

Those weren't the only oddities. She was strong. Stronger than a woman of her size should be. Fast, fast enough she'd caught a fish barehanded and laughed as she tossed it to him on shore. She liked to chase rabbits and even the occasional squirrel. And when he gave her a long kiss, her foot thumped the ground.

Maybe she'd been a dog in another life?

Now he was just being silly and probably overreacting. Athena would tell him her secret when she was good and ready. He just needed to be patient.

While she hung out with her sister, he headed into the city to check on things. His apartment appeared untouched. Perhaps they'd been paranoid for nothing.

Glancing around, he wondered if he should let the place go. Since he'd quit his job at the warehouse and transferred his firefighting volunteer status to his grandparents' township, he had no reason to keep paying. Not to mention, they couldn't live on the farm forever. As a couple, they needed their own space. A bedroom where he could make love to her and have her voice her enjoyment. A living room where they could snuggle on a couch watching what they liked rather than the nightly *Jeopardy* and *Wheel of Fortune*. A space where they could truly be themselves.

Perhaps on Athena's return, he'd suggest they look at renting a place in town. Then they could still be close enough to do chores and get paid—his grandparents believed in paying for a job well done. As Gramps said, *"Pay you or pay that idiot who takes twice as long? You're cheaper."*

Derek left his apartment after grabbing a few things and headed out to the street where he'd parked Gramps' truck. As he clambered into the driver's seat, he noticed a van parked across the road. Unmarked, windows tinted. Probably a service truck. Still, he kept eyeing it in his rearview mirror until he turned the corner. It didn't budge, and he laughed inwardly at his paranoia.

It had been weeks since Athena escaped. More than likely the doctor who took her had ceased his search and moved on to his next victim.

Which led to his other concern. Why wouldn't Athena go to the cops? Why didn't she want this doctor and his associates arrested? When he'd asked, she'd simply said, *"They're too smart to get caught. Even if they did listen, it would be my word against his."*

Derek returned to the farm and kept busy the rest of that day and night. Athena had asked him to fetch her in the morning at the same place.

He half expected her to not show, but to his

delight, when he entered the restaurant, she sat at a table and smiled in welcome.

She rose to greet him with a kiss before sitting again. "Breakfast?"

He'd already eaten but still sat and nodded. "How's your sister?"

"Good. Whole family is doing well." She paused. "I told them about you."

"Oh, and what did you say?"

"That I met a hot firefighter with an awesome dick and we've been fucking like bunnies."

He snorted. "Sounds about right."

"Actually, I said you were a really good guy and that we'd be over soon so you could meet them."

"Really?" He must have sounded surprised.

She appeared almost shy as she said, "Yeah. They were a bit shocked. I've never brought a guy over before. You'll be the first."

He just about burst hearing that. "Whenever you're ready, sugarplum. No rush."

Her lips curved. "You're always so understanding, and that makes me feel even worse for sending you away yesterday."

"I get it. You're protective of your family."

"And yet you had me meeting yours right away."

"Because of circumstances. Trust me, I usually would have kept you far from Grams."

"I adore her."

"And she likes you, which is a miracle."

"My family will love you as well. I guess I don't want you to think I was ashamed of you or something."

"Ashamed of the hot firefighter with an epic dick?"

Her laughter always warmed him. "I'm so glad we met."

Him too. But Derek couldn't get rid of a niggling fear. A fear she'd leave and he'd have to go back to his dull existence.

They ate and headed back for the farm, with him broaching the idea of them moving out. "What do you think of us getting our own place?"

"Move back to the city?"

"An option, or we could stick close to the farm."

"I do love working out there, and I never thought I'd say this, but I kind of miss the city. Your grams' cooking is awesome, don't get me wrong, but sometimes a girl craves surf and turf or some hand-rolled sushi, and Richmond isn't exactly a hot spot for takeout."

"Which explains in a nutshell why I moved out in the first place." He laughed. "If you want city, then while my apartment isn't huge, we could make it work until we found a bigger place."

She bit her lip. "You think it's safe?"

Time to come clean. "I popped in yesterday to check on it."

"You what?" she exclaimed.

"It's okay. Nothing was touched, and I didn't see anyone watching it."

She drummed her fingers on her leg. "You took a risk."

"We can't live in hiding forever," his soft reply.

"I know." She sighed. "But it's been so nice."

It had. So why was he trying to ruin it?

"We don't have to decide right away."

"Can I think about it?"

"Take all the time you need," he offered.

As he pulled into his grandparents' place, he noticed his cousin's car parked and groaned. "Not again."

"Are you kidding? Yay. I wonder what I can do to needle him this time." Athena took pleasure in taunting Frank. Kind of entertaining to watch since Frank usually had women eating out of his hand.

As Derek hit the first porch step, his phone pinged. He glanced at it. "Shit. I've got to go. There's a fire, and I'm being called into service."

"Go and save the world, honey. I'll be fine." She brushed her lips over his. "I'll be ready later to thank my hero."

Oh hell yeah. "Tell my grandparents where I've gone."

"Will do. Be careful," she murmured.

He would be because she was worth coming home to.

The fire proved to be a big one that started in an

old barn and then spread to the nearby fields. While mown of their corn, the dry stalks burned and emitted billowing black smoke.

Derek found himself digging a trench with others, back-breaking sweaty work in their heavy gear. The firebreak, though, helped to contain the fire, although it took a few hours.

Once they were done, they headed to the firehall, and Derek stood in line for a shower to sluice the worst of it from his skin. While the crew celebrated their victory with pizza, Derek headed out, eager to get back to the farm and Athena.

Only something was wrong.

Frank's car had been smacked by something in the long laneway and sat halfway across the drive. The driver's side gaped open and showed the air bag deployed.

Derek frowned and checked his phone. No signal.

At all.

Not normal. Since he couldn't budge Frank's car, he exited his vehicle and ran. Ignored his aching muscles, ignored everything in the face of his sudden fear.

He pounded up to the house, and as he threw open the door, the first thing he heard was Frank yelling, "Don't kill me."

He found his cousin in the kitchen, tied to a chair, Grams standing in front of him, looking grim, sporting a black eye, and holding her meat tenderizer.

Gramps sat in a chair, ice pack to his jaw, rifle between his legs, also glaring at Frank.

A sinking feeling hit Derek as he growled, "What happened? Where's Athena?"

Even before Grams opened her mouth, Derek knew. "The fuckers got her, and it's all Frank's fault."

CHAPTER 11

ATHENA WATCHED DEREK LEAVE THE FARM TO fight a fire and wished she could go with him. She'd missed him. It had been the first time in a month they'd not slept together. However, her furry secret didn't give her a choice. It used to be the arrival of the full moon filled her with joy. She would shift and run, chasing the night away.

But Dr. Rogers and Derek had changed all that. She feared either of them learning her secret. If Rogers exposed her, then life as she knew it would be over. With Derek, if he found out, would he accept her lycanthropy? Because if he didn't, she might have to do the unthinkable. Well, she probably wouldn't. Ares would handle it for her if she asked, but she really hoped it never came to that. Really hoped the bond they'd built could withstand the fact she was more than human.

She still remembered her dad having the talk with them at a young age about how it was imperative they never tell anyone. To which she'd replied, *"Mom knows."*

"I had no choice but to tell her because, from birth, you shifted on the full moon. You should have heard her scream when she found a wolf pup in the crib. Luckily, your mom is awesome."

"What if she'd not been?" she'd asked.

His lips had turned down. *"We wouldn't be the family we are today."*

Despite his love for Mom, he'd have done whatever it took to keep Athena safe. And she could do no less for her family. *Please don't let it come to that.*

Those thoughts chased her that night as she ran with her sister, in a place a fair distance from home, where no one could see them. An abandoned property, the house long boarded and not visible from the road.

Her distraction had her stumbling into a stream and snorting out water. Missing the fat rabbit that hopped in her path. Lying down and sighing in the moonlight.

Her actions didn't go unnoticed.

The next morning, once they'd flipped back into human skin, her sister called her out as they dressed in the clothes they'd left in the trunk of Selene's car.

"What's got you looking so mopey?" Selene asked as they drove back to town. "I thought you said everything was okay."

"Better than okay. Great. I'm just tired."

"Are you? Has something happened? Is this about the doctor?"

"I haven't seen or heard anything since I left the city."

"Then this must be about the guy who rescued you."

"Hardly rescued."

"Nice avoidance and clarification. You're pining over the boyfriend."

"I don't pine."

"It's not a crime to admit you miss him."

"How can I miss him when we've only been apart a day?"

"In that case, since it's no big deal, spend the day at the farm. We can sneak you in. That tiny visit with Mom yesterday was barely enough to catch up. And you missed Ares entirely since he was at work until dinner." They'd left late afternoon to ensure they didn't have a tail for their nocturnal jaunt. Ares had stuck around and hid himself in the basement to keep an ear on their mother.

"It's too risky."

"Not if we put you in the trunk again where no one can see you," Selene countered.

"I can't. Derek's coming to pick me up around nine."

"Text him and ask him to come later."

When Athena bit her lip, trying to figure out an excuse, Selene sang, "Athena's in love."

"Am not!" Was she? No denying she couldn't wait to see him. Thought of him constantly.

"I cannot wait to meet the guy who finally has you acting like a schoolgirl," Selene crowed while laughing.

"I'm almost thirty. Hardly a child," Athena had pointed out.

"Fine, you're a grown-ass woman who is giddy in love." Selena slapped the steering wheel and snorted. "Hot damn he must be special."

"He is," her soft admission.

"When can we meet him?"

"When it's safe."

"And how will you know it's safe to come out of hiding?"

Athena had no clue. They'd had no issues at the farm. Not at his grandparents' or her family's. The dark web posting with a bounty appeared to have disappeared, or at least didn't show anywhere Derek looked. But as he noted, he didn't have access to all the forums or message boards.

Could it be that Dr. Rogers gave up? He didn't seem the type, but then again, she'd chosen to not go after him. Her plans for revenge evaporated in the face of her burgeoning relationship with Derek.

Derek...

"You're doing it again," Selene had accused.

"Doing what?"

"Getting that doe-eyed look on your face. You were thinking of him."

"Fine. I was. I like him. A lot."

"I knew it," Selene huffed, again slapping the steering wheel.

"You're annoying," was Athena's grumble.

"I know. It's my job as your little sister."

"Can we change the subject?"

They'd talked about minor stuff. Selene's frustration with the dating world. Ares having broken the heart of yet another woman. Mom's upcoming trip to Mexico.

Their hug had been tight when Selene dropped Athena off not far from the restaurant. Athena had chosen a window seat so she could see him pull in. The smile that stretched her lips at the sight of Derek was tempered by the trepidation on his face.

Was he mad?

His expression flipped to pure joy when he saw her.

He'd missed her too. Not just missed her. On the drive back, he'd broached them moving in together. For the first time in her life, Athena wanted to take that big step. Heck, they'd technically been cohabiting for the last month, although it felt more like a holiday since they were guests of his grandparents. Might be time for them to truly take a shot at this.

She'd tell him when he got back from fighting his fire. The rumble of his departing truck faded, and she eyed the house. Her melancholy would probably be improved by needling his cousin.

Athena entered the farmhouse to find Frank sitting in the kitchen with Gramps, having a coffee. Grams stood at the counter, stiff-lipped as she rolled out some dough.

"There you are." Frank's greeting with a smile much too bright. "I was hoping to see you."

Athena ignored him to address Gramps. "Derek told me to let you know he got called in for a fire and took the truck."

"Guess we won't be going to the yarn store," Gramps announced with fake chagrin.

Grams glared. "I swear you do on purpose each time I wanna go."

"Hey, this wasn't my fault."

Frank dangled his keys. "You're welcome to borrow my wheels. I'll hang with Athena while you go."

"I ain't driving that foreign car," Gramps declared. "Hybrid bullshit. In the apocalypse, there won't be any charging stations. Gas vehicles will be key. Especially the kind without all those fancy bullshit electronics."

"If you change your mind..." Frank tossed the keys to the table.

"Never!"

Athena bit her lip lest she ruin Gramps' indignation. "I'll go check on the horses since Derek's out this afternoon," Athena offered.

Gramps nodded. "You know where the feed is. I'll be out in a minute to give you a hand. Just waiting for the pot brownie to kick in." His idea of pain management being of the herbal variety.

As Athena went to leave, Frank suddenly joined her. "I'll give you a hand."

"I don't need one," she muttered.

"Then company," he insisted, tagging along to the barn.

"Don't you have better things to do?"

"I thought we could get to know each other better."

"Why?" she rudely asked.

"Well, you are dating my cousin." A sound reason, yet something niggled. Frank appeared smug and nervous at the same time.

As they strode into the barn, she reached for the light switch and flipped it. Nothing came on.

"Power's out," she noted.

"Probably a breaker."

She opened the doors wide to give herself as much daylight as possible and noticed Frank's grimace at the pungent scent of animal. It didn't bother her. Everyone and everything had a smell. That of a horse was a lot more natural than whatever godawful cologne Frank wore.

As she grabbed the first bucket and filled it, Frank felt a need to make conversation.

"How's things with you and Derek?"

"None of your business."

"Just looking out for my coz."

"Are you? Because the way I hear it you tend to butt heads more often than not."

"I think it's because he can't handle my success."

Athena snorted. "Pretty sure that's not it." Then, because she hoped to make him leave, added, "I hear it's because you have a thing for making passes at his girlfriends."

"Is it my fault they throw themselves at me?"

"I highly doubt that," she muttered.

"Not my fault I'm so good-looking and well-endowed."

Wait, had he actually said that?

She couldn't help but laugh. "Bless your heart for thinking that, but I can tell you right now who the bigger man is." In more than one way.

He didn't appreciate her reply, judging by his scowl. "How long you planning to hide out on the farm?"

"Who says I'm hiding?"

"Please. We both know you don't belong out here. You've got city written all over you."

She hung the bucket on the hook for the mare before turning to retort, "I was born and raised on a farm."

"And left it."

"I did, but not because I hated it." She couldn't

have said why she wanted to argue with Frank, other than he just grated on every single one of her nerves.

"So, you're not hiding?" he insisted.

"Why would you think I am?"

"Because a little birdie might have told me there's a bounty out on your head."

Athena froze in the act of filling the next bucket with oats and a few apples. "Seems unlikely, as I've committed no crime."

"Never said it was a police bounty. There are people interested in you, and they're offering a pretty penny."

She took a second to compose her features before she turned to face him. "Why don't you spit out what you think you know?"

"I know that we're supposed to keep your presence a secret. Derek made that very clear." Said on a sour note.

"Abusive ex," she stated as a plausible reason.

"Must be a rich one, given what he's offering to find you. Surprised you'd choose my cousin over someone with money. Or is he just a temporary fling? Trying to make the old flame jealous? Maybe up the price so you and Derek can cash in?"

Athena had enough of Frank's mouth and attitude. Before he could blink, she had him on his back, a knee pressed to his chest, an arm over his throat. "You really are a piece of work, aren't you?" she said softly.

"Let me up."

"I think not. You came here for a reason, and I'm going to guess it's because you saw an easy payday."

"Maybe I'm concerned about my family?" he huffed. "I don't believe it's an ex-boyfriend looking for you. You're hiding here because you're a wanted woman. You can't deny it. I've seen the picture, and all I've got to do to collect the twenty K is tell them where you are."

Her blood ran cold. They'd upped the ante, meaning Rogers had not given up. She'd just disappeared a little too well, so he sweetened the pot.

"Did you tell them where I was?" she growled.

"That's going to depend on you," Frank chirped, suddenly thinking he had the upper hand once more.

"I'm not fucking you," she stated flatly.

"As if your pussy is worth twenty grand," he scoffed. "More like giving you a chance to outbid. Make it worth my while and I'll keep my mouth shut."

"Or I could shut it for you," she offered. "I hear a broken jaw takes about six months to heal. How do you feel about slurping shakes for that long?"

"Threatening me? Wait until I tell Grams. She'll kick your ass off the farm."

"Go ahead." She rose from Frank and waved a hand. "Why don't you go tell Grams and Gramps how you're blackmailing me? Or better yet, why not tattle to Derek? He's itching for a reason to knock your teeth out."

"It's not blackmail. Just offering you a chance to make a better deal."

She arched a brow. "I'm not some dummy you can gaslight. You are blackmailing me, and I'm telling you right now, it won't fly. Not to mention, you'll have nothing to tell since I won't be where you say I am."

"Going to leave my cousin in the lurch?"

Derek. Fuck. She couldn't flee without talking to him. Then again, he'd insist on joining her. Which might not be bad. Running wouldn't suck as much with her lover by her side.

"How about you—" She paused midsentence as she heard a vehicle coming up the drive. She glanced at Frank. "Did you already open your fat mouth?"

"Nooo." A long drawn-out syllable.

She pursed her lips. "Why does it sound like you're lying?"

"I didn't tell them where you were," he whined, but she noticed the perspiration at his temples.

"What did you say? What have you told them?" she hissed.

"Nothing, just asked if there was a bonus if I brought you in myself."

"As if you could take me," she muttered, but more worrisome, he'd implied to the person posting the bounty that he knew where to find her. Had that led to them following Frank?

Could be whoever parked out front was unrelated to her situation. Not a chance she could take.

She glanced at Frank, who'd risen to his feet and appeared pale.

"You stay here," she ordered.

"You can't tell me what—"

Smack. She hit hard enough he reeled. Another good hook to the jaw and he was out cold.

One less idiot to handle.

She exited the barn and snuck up to the house via the rear, the driveway out of her line of sight. Several car doors slammed, but she'd only heard one car. Could be visitors. Should she take a peek to see if she panicked for nothing?

A male voice spoke, but she couldn't quite make out the words at this distance. Hearing the crunch of gravel, she ducked behind the chicken coop as a guy in combats with no badging sauntered into the yard. The guy scanned the area before his lips moved, obviously reporting.

So not a friendly visitor.

Fuck and double fuck.

The options were limited. She could run, take off on foot with no supplies, not even her phone, which she'd left in the house. Or confront whoever waited inside.

Or...

She remembered the keys Frank had tossed on the kitchen table. If she could get her hands on those, she'd have wheels. Her phone was charging on the kitchen counter as well. She'd have no cash, but she could at least send Derek and her family messages. However, that plan required her taking out the guy guarding the yard.

She couldn't sneak up on him. He'd see her coming the moment she popped out from behind the coop. How to distract him? And quickly. The front door had slammed shut, meaning whoever visited had gone inside with Grams and Gramps. She could only hope they weren't all talk and could handle themselves. It helped that she knew they wanted her and not them.

The clucking of the hens gave her an idea. Ronnie the rooster sat atop the coop. Not allowed in with his ladies but that didn't stop him from keeping an eye on them as they pecked away.

"Sorry, Grams," she muttered as she waited for the guy to look the opposite way before unlatching the side gate. It swung open, and she ducked away just in time.

A glance showed the guy frowning at the coop, most likely wondering if he'd miss its open door. Out strutted a chicken, a scrawny one who liked to peck if she saw you going for her eggs. Another followed. They spread out from the coop, necks bobbing, looking for food.

Ronnie fluttered down to watch over his flock, which moved toward the back door, sensing or smelling the bucket of grain kept just inside.

The guy shooed at the hen that waddled too close.

Ronnie took exception.

The rooster let out a sound and flapped his stubby wings as he went after the guy. The fellow could have shot it, or probably even given it a good kick but, like most people, had a brain fart when confronted by something small, feathery, and hostile. He stepped away. Ronnie darted in. The guy retreated some more and shouted into his mic, "There's a fucking bird attacking me."

He moved around the corner of the farmhouse, rooster in chase, giving Athena the opening she needed.

The kitchen door didn't creak as Athena slipped in, and she shut it just as quietly to avoid being heard. The kitchen seemed awfully silent, and a glance at the stove showed no display. The power was off in the house, too. Might explain why they'd had no warning, seeing how Grams had motion detectors and cameras set up to watch those entering the property.

Seeing the car keys on the table, she wrapped her fist around them lest they jingle, and stuffed them into her pocket, along with her phone. The murmur of voices drew her to the hall where she could hear a male voice in the living room.

A voice she knew.

Dr. Rogers tried to cajole Grams and Gramps into revealing her presence.

"Are you sure? I have it on good authority you have a woman staying here. Name of Athena. Platinum-blonde hair, although she might have dyed it. Twenty-nine but could pass for younger. I believe she's involved with your grandson."

"Nope. Wrong farm. Our Derek's single," Grams announced.

"And gay," Gramps added. "Likes the boys, he does."

Athena slapped a hand over her mouth lest she laugh at the lie.

"You should know Athena is dangerous. Not the type of person you want around." Rogers changed tactics.

"And who are you?" Grams asked. "Barging into our home. Being rude."

"I'm someone you don't want to mess with." Rogers' flat reply.

"What are you, a cop?" Gramps barked. "Let's see a badge. Or better yet a warrant."

"I don't need those because the people I work for don't officially exist, but let me assure you, they have clout. Enough clout to seize this farm from under you."

"Doubt a judge would go along with it," Gramps argued.

"Did I mention they buy judges all the time? Is Athena really worth losing your livelihood and home?"

"If I knew her, which I don't, I'd say she's probably worth saving if it pisses off the likes of you. Rude little fucker, coming into my home and making threats after calling me a liar. Git," Grams spat. "Git before I load you full of buckshot."

"It's like you want me to hurt you." Dr. Rogers sighed. "I take no pleasure in it, just so you know. However, my work is too important to have a pair of hillbillies standing in my way. So either tell me where to find Athena or this conversation is about to get ugly."

"Fucking prick." Gramps' chair creaked. "You've got a lot of nerve. Now git your ass and that of your goon off my property before I put a hole in them." So not just Rogers in the living room.

"I'm not leaving without Athena."

Click-click. Someone was armed.

"You don't want to do that," Rogers replied softly.

"Try me, asshole."

Zap. A taser went off—a sound she well knew since they'd used it on her a few times while in captivity. The sounds of a scuffle erupted, grunting, the smacking of flesh, an exhalation of pain, and Grams yelling, "Motherfucker."

Athena ran into the room to find Grams holding the fireplace poker and a guy in combats lying prone on the floor, but more worrisome, Rogers stood over a dazed Gramps, the electrodes from the taser still attached to his chest. Gramps had his eyes closed, and his breathing appeared ragged.

"Move away from Gramps," Athena growled.

Grams, despite one eye swelling shut, waved the poker and yelled, "Run, Athena. We'll hold them off."

As if Athena would leave them to Rogers' mercy. "Here I am, Doctor. Come and get me." She beckoned with her fingers.

Rogers arched a brow. "Do you think me dumb? March your ass into the van parked out front, or I kill the old man. I upped the voltage. Next push of the button and he's frying."

Athena held up her hands. "I'll go with you but leave these folks alone."

"In that case... after you." Rogers indicated the front door.

Athena began walking. She had no choice. The thing she'd worried about had come to pass. She'd dragged innocent people into her shit, and they'd gotten hurt.

Rogers smirked as she passed him. "Did you really think you could hide from me forever? Count yourself lucky I found you, because my next step was to grab your siblings to see if they share your genetics."

"They don't."

"You do realize their blood will tell."

"Leave them alone," she growled.

"I will so long as you behave. See, I don't need all of you, just one for proof, and given you and I have a history, I want it to be you by my side when I tell the world exactly what you are."

"She's a good girl, unlike you, you prick," Grams

retorted. She'd inched close enough to swing her poker.

The blow didn't knock Rogers out, but he did stumble. Gramps, who'd been playing possum, ripped the barbs from the taser free and rolled, if awkwardly, to his feet.

"Gramps, get Grams out of here." Athena didn't take her eyes from Rogers, who looked entirely too confident. Might be because he had Gramps' gun in hand and his goon was stirring.

"I ain't running," Grams protested.

Which meant Athena had to. She had to lead Rogers away from here lest he take them hostage again.

Athena laced her hands on her head. "I'll go with you so long as you leave these folks alone."

"Finally, you're seeing sense," Rogers boasted. "And they say old bitches can't learn new tricks."

The slur pursed Athena's lips, but she didn't rise to his baiting. She glanced at the good people who'd harbored her and murmured, "Thank you for everything. Sorry I brought trouble to your doorstep."

Grams looked pissed. "Don't apologize. I promised you'd be safe."

"Ah yes, your piddly security system. All it took was cutting the power," Rogers boasted.

"The generator should have kicked in," Grams' sullen reply. Only it was waiting on a part. Athena had heard Grams yelling at the company that kept promising its delivery.

"Let's go. Enough dawdling." Rogers waved the barrel of the shotgun.

The goon on the floor groaned and rose, glaring at Grams.

She bared her teeth in reply.

"Tell Derek..." What message could Athena give? None. He'd be crushed. Pissed. And the last thing she needed was for him to come looking for her. "Tell him I'm sorry," she whispered as she headed out the door.

Out front, an unmarked van sat waiting with its side door open. Frank's car sat parked beside it.

A guy sat in the driver's seat of the van. A glance to her left showed the other one farther away, still trying to escape the angry cock.

"Move it," Rogers barked.

"If you insist," she muttered, suddenly whirling and shoving at Rogers on the step behind her. He reeled and fell into his goon, the pair of them tumbling in a heap of limbs and yelling.

Athena bolted for Frank's car, the door unlocked. The push-start button responded to the remote in her pocket, and the engine roared to life. She gunned the car and spun the wheel, flipping it around before tearing up the driveway, kicking up dust and gravel.

A peek in the rearview showed a cloud of dust but also movement. The dull glow of headlights showed Rogers coming after Athena.

Good.

At this point, it was less about her getting away than ensuring Grams' and Gramps' safety.

She raced the narrow track to the road, only to curse as she saw another vehicle heading at her.

Another unmarked van and no room for them both.

She couldn't go back; she couldn't turn.

She closed her eyes and pressed the gas, hoping, praying, the other driver would chicken out first.

Wham.

The impact deployed the airbags, punching her in the face, hard enough her dazed butt didn't fight when the door got yanked open. Rough hands yanked her out and had her cuffed before she could focus her eyes.

She got tossed into a van, and the sedative injected into her arm knocked her out before they'd slammed the door shut.

When she woke it was to find herself in a cell.

Afraid, yes, but not for herself.

Because she wasn't here alone. Her family was with her.

CHAPTER 12

ATHENA GRABBED THE BARS TO HER CAGE AND stared at her sister imprisoned across from her. Beside Selene, in her own locked box, Mom.

"No. Oh no," Athena cried. "What happened?"

Mom's lips turned down. "I thought they were the cable crew coming to fix the internet, so I let them in. A mistake since I woke here with your sister."

"What of Ares?" Athena asked, not seeing her brother.

"He wasn't home, so I'm hoping they didn't nab him."

Selene wasn't smiling, a rarity. "I can't believe I didn't sniff out the ambush. I walked downstairs because the guy yelled something about Mom falling. As I walked past him, he jabbed me with a needle."

"They tracked me down at Derek's grandparents'

farm. Fuck me." Athena paced. "I'm so stupid. This is my fault. I should have done something about Roger."

"It's not your fault, baby girl," Mom soothed. "It had been weeks. We all thought he'd given up."

"Turns out he was just biding his time," Athena grumbled. "Fuck!" Frustration had her clenching her fists. Despite what Mom said, she was to blame. She should have forced her family to move. Disappeared entirely from Ontario and started anew. She should have not been so caught up in playing the happy couple with Derek and stuck to her plan of revenge. If she'd killed Rogers—

"Don't!" Mom snapped.

"Don't what?" she muttered.

"Don't play the woulda-coulda-shoulda game. We had no way of knowing this would happen."

"But I did know," Athena huffed. "And instead of nipping it in the bud, I played ostrich, hiding my head in the sand, pretending like it never happened. And now look at us."

"Have faith, baby girl."

"Faith in what?" she cried. Her mom truly didn't grasp how bad this was, her fault for glossing over her captivity. She'd not wanted to traumatize her mother with her experience.

"Your brother is still out there. He'll come for us."

"With what army? Rogers has guards coming out the ass."

"He'll find a way. And if he doesn't, you or Selene will. After all, you escaped once before."

She had. Barely.

A *hum* and a *click* led to a door opening.

Rogers sauntered into the room, and the sight of him unleashed her rage.

Athena yelled, "You fucking prick. You promised you'd leave them alone, but meanwhile, you already had them in your clutches."

"I lied." And he was quite smug about it.

"What happened to just needing me for proof?" she huffed.

"Also a lie. I mean, one lycanthrope is amazing, but a whole family?" He spread his hands. "That's terrifying because it will make people wonder if their neighbors and friends have a secret."

"I should have killed you," she muttered. "Should have known you'd never give up."

"Of course I didn't give up, silly bitch. I was delayed. Your escape forced me to move the lab, hence why you got a reprieve. My new one is not as central as the last." He made a moue of discontent. "My commute has doubled, but finding a private location with the space and power needed for the equipment proved tricky. Ironically, we're not far from where I found you."

"Now what?" she snapped.

"Now, we plan your grand unveiling as we wait for the full moon. I'm thinking TD Place. Under the lights. We'll charge a nominal fee for the tickets. I'm going to call it, The Wolves in Human Clothing exhibition. It will be grand. Those watching will be skeptical, hence the big splashy event. Big screens that never pan away from you as the moon emerges. Everyone will see you change. Become a monster."

"There's only one monster in this room, and it's not my daughters," Mom's soft retort.

"You might have been a waste of time capturing. Given the prelims on your bloodwork, I'm going to guess the father was the contributing factor to your genetic anomaly."

Mom clamped her lips shut.

"No need to answer. The thorough bloodwork will soon reveal all. I can't wait to separate the human from the lycanthrope. Although we'll have to make do with DNA samples for your paternal side, given the father is dead."

"Good luck with that. We had my husband cremated," Mom spat.

"Doesn't matter. A comparison of your DNA will give us the truth. Now get some rest. We've got a busy month ahead preparing. And don't worry. There won't be any mishaps like last time. No more stupid, randy guards delivering food." He pointed to the slot in the cage big enough for a tray of food and nothing else. "Until tomorrow, when we start the tests."

Rogers left, and Athena's forehead hit the bars as

she closed her eyes and tried to not lose her ever-loving mind. Fucking hell.

"Don't worry, baby girl. I'm sure Ares is working on a way to get us out."

Athena eyed her mother. "How, when he has no idea where we are?" Her lips turned down. "This is my fault. I should have taken out Rogers when I had the chance."

"You're not a killer," Mom stated.

"I could be," Athena's dark reply.

"Can we talk about something else? Because I, for one, am not letting that pencil dick ruin my mood. I saw your new boyfriend," Selene chirped. "What a cutie."

"How?" Athena asked with a frown.

"Because I stuck around and saw you having breakfast. Talk about dreamy." Selene fanned herself.

"You spied!" Athena exclaimed.

Mom shook her head. "I told you not to tell her. But your sister is right. He's a handsome boy. She showed me pics."

"Man, Mom. He's thirty-three."

"And a firefighter," Selene added with an approving nod. "The kind sexy enough to pose for a month in one of them calendars."

"Can we not talk about Derek? I'd rather not think about the fact I'll never see him again."

"Don't be so pessimistic."

"We're in a cage," Athena reminded her Pollyanna

sister. "A locked cage, under surveillance." She waved a hand to the camera watching. "In a place crawling with guards."

"Have a little faith," Selene declared.

"Faith in my ability to screw things up?" Athena sighed. "Sorry. I don't mean to be a Debbie Downer, just Jeezus, we are so fucked. I should have known he'd come after you. We should have run the moment I escaped."

"Your dad used to say when you can't hide anymore, fight until your last breath."

"Or let the fucker expose us and stop pretending we're something we're not," Selene chirped. "I mean, people love Fred, the Sasquatch."

"He's a sideshow freak."

"For now. There are people trying to free him. There's a petition making the rounds and a court challenge."

"Challenging what?"

"That Fred is sentient enough that caging him is, in a sense, slavery, which is illegal."

"Hasn't worked for monkeys," Athena pointed out.

"Yet," Selene insisted. "But it's coming. The world is changing. Becoming more diversified."

"Cultural diversity is a hell of a lot different from people who change into wolves."

"But there's the key word. People. We are human. Just with a little something extra."

"We shouldn't be talking about this." Not that it mattered. Rogers knew what she was. Knew it and soon would show the world.

Show Derek.

Would he remember her fondly, or would she become the mistake he'd almost succumbed to?

She'd probably never find out.

CHAPTER 13

DEREK JUST ABOUT LOST HIS MIND. ARRIVING not even twenty minutes after everything went down to see his grandparents injured scared the fuck out of him. They could have died. It also made him mad, because who the fuck attacked folks in their seventies?

Knowing Athena had been taken crushed him. He'd not been around to protect her, and now she was gone.

The only good thing to come out of this mess? Frank was finally persona non grata.

The fucker, who'd been tied to a chair, had the nerve to whine, "Your bitch girlfriend hit me."

Derek offered him a stiff, "I'm sure she had a good reason."

"She's psycho that's why," blurted Frank.

"Say that again," Derek growled, his fists clenched.

The urge to hit something rode him hard, and who better than his smug cousin?

"She attacked me for no reason."

"I doubt that," Derek muttered before adding, "And in case you hadn't noticed, we've got bigger problems than your little boo-boo. Grams and Gramps were attacked." He didn't add Athena had been kidnapped. Frank would probably say something dumb, and then Derek would have to kill him.

Frank's lips turned down. "Wasn't expecting that to happen."

"What's that supposed to mean?" a bristling Derek retorted.

Grams had figured it out, though, hence why Frank was bound to a chair. She glared and hissed, "You fucking piece of shit. How dare you betray this family."

"Dare what? I didn't do nothing," Frank complained.

"Liar. You knew those thugs were coming. The driveway alarms should have gone off, even without power since they're on a battery backup. Someone tampered with them. The same someone who offered to go to the basement to fetch me a new jar of jam after he accidentally knocked the open one off the counter." Under her unrelenting scowl, Frank squirmed and fessed up.

"I didn't expect them to get rough."

"Them who?" Derek barked. Derek had gone beyond rage. He was now cold. Stone. Fucking. Cold.

"I don't know." Frank shrugged. "They didn't post a name, just a reward to whoever had information on Athena's location."

A good thing Gramps held him back because Frank would have died in that moment. "You fucking son of a bitch. You sold her out!"

"You would have, too, for twenty K."

"No, I wouldn't have. No person with any kind of empathy or fucking morals would," Derek snapped.

"I don't see the big deal. She's mixed up in some shady business. You should thank me for finding out before you got dragged into whatever mess she's involved in." Frank tried to justify, but Grams wasn't having it.

"You're not welcome here," she stated. "Git out and don't come back." She grabbed a knife and sliced at the tape holding him.

"You're gonna kick me out over a stranger?" Frank had a surprised Pikachu face.

"No, we're kicking you out because you're a scum-sucking low-life. Lord knows, I've tried to be understanding. Tried to look past your many faults, but this..." Gramps shook his head. "This is the last straw."

"Is this because they roughed you up? I swear I didn't know that would happen."

"Git out before I smash your smug face." Grams was done talking and threatened with the meat tenderizer.

"Gramps—"

"You heard my wife. Out, and don't ever come back, because if you do…" Gramps left the threat open-ended.

Frank opened his mouth, and Derek stepped in. "Let's go. You heard them."

"But—"

Derek quite enjoyed grabbing Frank by the scruff and literally tossing him off the front porch.

That small pleasure didn't last.

Athena was missing and in danger. Worse, he didn't have the slightest idea where to start looking so he could save her.

He tried, though, scouring the dark web for any mention of the bounty. Cursing himself for not having seen the one Frank spotted. Mad that he'd been fighting fires instead of defending his family and lover.

He had no appetite for the food Grams had brewing in the crockpot, no one did, and they were all on edge when Gramps muttered, "Someone's coming up the drive."

Gramps had flipped the power back on, meaning the security system was online. Grams held out her phone so Derek could peek at the vehicle approaching. A blue pickup truck he didn't recognize.

"You stay here. I'll go see who it is."

"Don't you worry. We've got your back." Grams had a shotgun gripped tight, and Gramps held his rifle. It killed him to see them shaken. To see them finally realize they weren't the brawlers of their youth anymore, but old folk.

Derek headed for the front door and stood arms crossed on the porch as the truck parked and a big dude emerged.

"Who are you? What do you want?" Not exactly the most polite of greetings, but given Derek's shit day and mood, the best anyone was getting.

"You Derek?" asked the guy, eyeing him up and down.

"Who's asking?"

"Athena's brother."

The response shot up Derek's brows. "Ares?"

"Yeah. Where's my sister?"

"Not here." An admission that almost stuck in his throat.

"Where is she? I need to talk to her right now."

"I don't know." Derek slumped. "She was taken a few hours ago."

"Fuck!" Ares turned and kicked the tires of his truck while letting out a litany of curses Grams would have admired.

"Sorry. I should have been here, but I was called in to fight a fire. My grandparents did their best to protect her, but Rogers came with some goons."

"Busy little fucker," Ares spat. "He also took my mom and sister while I was at work."

"Oh shit," Derek muttered.

"Yeah, shit for Rogers because I'm going to fuck him up good. I was hoping to have Athena as backup, but guess I'll have to go alone."

"Not alone. I'll help."

"As will we." Grams and Gramps stepped out behind him.

Ares blinked. Probably wasn't used to seeing an old lady toting a gun with a knife strapped to her hip.

The man shook his head. "I appreciate the offer, but this is going to be ugly."

"It already is ugly. Those fuckers came here, beat on my grandparents, took Athena, and also kidnapped her family. That kind of shit ain't cool. Not one bit. And if we can figure out where they are, I want to be there helping with the rescue and beatdown."

"It might get bloody," Ares warned.

"So be it. They struck the first blow. Time to show them why that was a bad idea." Derek always wondered if he had a killer gene. Grams and Gramps certainly did. His dad... not so much. But apparently, Derek just needed the right motivation.

"I could use the help. I ain't exactly Rambo." Ares raked his fingers through his hair. "We'll need a plan. The place they're in, while remote, is guarded."

The words hit, and Derek blurted out, "Wait, you know where they are?"

Ares nodded. "After Athena went missing without a trace that first time, I had us chipped." He held up his wrist. "Think of it as an air tag but for people. Athena doesn't have one yet, but I imagine she's being held in the same place as my mom and Selene."

"Holy shit." Hope suddenly blossomed.

Grams clapped her hands. "This calls for some sticky pudding and coffee. Git inside, boy. We've got some planning to do." She eyed Gramps. "We'll need Big Bessie ready to go. Load her up."

"Big Bessie?" Ares questioned.

"Armored vehicle with mounted gun," Gramps explained. "Good for smashing into things and can also withstand heavy fire."

"We'll also bring some grenades and other explosives in case we need to blast our way in," Grams added.

"Hold on, you have explosives?" Ares asked in a high-pitched voice.

"And flamethrowers and assault weapons." Grams rolled her eyes. "I swear I don't understand why more people aren't prepared for the apocalypse. Does no one see what's going on in the world?" She kept ranting as she entered the house with Gramps.

Ares cocked his head, looking puzzled. "Is your grandma always that gung-ho about going to war?"

"Dude, my grams has been ready since she was born."

"Well fuck. Guess this might not be a suicide mission after all," an incredulous Ares stated.

"We'll get them back," Derek promised, because the alternative, a life without Athena, wasn't something he even wanted to contemplate.

CHAPTER 14

ATHENA PACED THE CONFINES OF HER CAGE, seeking any weakness in the seams or bars. The welds were solid, the metal too thick to bend. The padlock unpickable. Her clothes had been stripped from her, leaving her in the dreaded scrubs.

After Rogers left, they didn't see anyone until dinnertime when a soldier, his face expressionless and grim, arrived with three flimsy plastic trays that he slid through the slots.

Once he left, Selene grimaced. "Microwave dinners? Really? That's almost as cruel as this cage. Not to mention no fork. What are we supposed to do, eat our mashed potatoes with our fingers?"

"Or slurp it like an animal. Cutlery can be used as a weapon, hence why we don't get any." Athena remained familiar with how captivity under Rogers worked.

"Good thing we'll be out of here soon," Selene chirped. "I've got leftover cheesecake in the fridge at home."

Athena admired her sister's optimism even if misplaced. Let her keep hope for as long as she could. Athena wished she could share it, but it appeared the doctor had moved locations. The stone cellar older and more rustic than that at the Experimental Farm. Large too, the pillars of wood and stacked cinder blocks rising as sentinels to break up the space. She saw no sign of whatever used to be in place before, unless the ductwork counted. There were cameras pointed at the cages, watching every move and listening to their every word. Other than the cages, there was a staircase, the treads of each riser thick wood, a few stacked crates, and the dreaded contraption Rogers used to call the rack. It was as bad as it sounded. A fourth cage remained empty, and she prayed it stayed that way.

"I hope Ares was smart enough to hide once he found out you were gone," Athena stated, poking at the meat that looked nothing like turkey. More like a hunk of rubber smothered in a thick brown sauce.

"He wouldn't have found out until dinnertime when he got off work. I wish we could have found a way to warn him." Mom ignored her tray and instead sat huddled.

"I don't know how you did it," Selene declared. "A whole month of this? I'd have been skin and bones, not to mention completely bonkers, by the time I escaped."

"It wasn't easy," Athena admitted.

"Did it hurt much?" Selene asked, her tone more somber than usual. "I mean, whatever stuff they did while they had you."

"Depended on the test. The needles and skin scrapings were easy to handle, but Rogers also kept doing stuff to see how I'd react. Like exposing me to hot and cold extremes. Intentionally bruising me to test my healing speed. He had me running on a treadmill like a hamster for hours on end."

"Ugh. I wouldn't last five minutes." Selene, while slim, hated exercise. She preferred to simply eat right to maintain her body weight.

"Were you molested?" Mom's stark question, one she'd shied from asking before.

"No, that's the one thing he didn't subject me to. Although he did harvest some of my eggs." Bragged about how much they'd be worth once he proved her lycanthropy.

The lights went out abruptly, and Selene squeaked.

"It's okay," Athena soothed. "It's our signal to go to sleep."

"Sleep how? No mattress or even a blanket." Athena could practically see Selene's pout.

"Try. We'll most likely have a long day tomorrow."

A day of being treated like lab rats.

Like Selene, Athena struggled to rest. She blamed

herself for the situation. Missed Derek. Worried about him. Fretted about Ares. Wanted to cry for her mom and sister. If only she'd tried harder to locate Rogers. Without him, perhaps they would have been safe.

She must have fallen asleep at some point since she had to blink bleary eyes as the lights suddenly illuminated, shining through her eyelids with stark brilliance.

A different guard, his expression just as blank as the last, brought them each a cardboard bowl of porridge, thick paste that she choked down. She needed to keep up her strength.

Selene complained. "No brown sugar or berries? What kind of torture is this?"

"Are the accommodations not to your liking?" Rogers' sudden appearance at the bottom of the stairs had Athena tensing.

"This isn't fit for a dog," Selene declared, pointing to it.

"Would you prefer raw meat?"

"Ew, no. Although some bacon would be nice. Along with some eggs. Home fries, too, if you have them."

"This is not a hotel," Rogers barked.

"Obviously, or you'd have better amenities. Right now I rate you zero stars." Selene kept poking Rogers.

"Mouthy little thing, aren't you? Tell you what. You want better food, and other things to improve your stay, then you simply need to cooperate. Shift."

Selene purposely ignored his request and pointed to the corner. "This plastic bucket you've left us won't do at all. I demand a proper bathroom."

"Change into your wolf," Rogers snapped. "Show me your furry side and we'll see about improving your situation."

"Me, a wolf?" Selene giggled. "That's the silliest thing I've ever heard. Have you been reading too much Stephenie Meyer? Next thing I know you'll be accusing us of being sparkly vampires."

Rogers turned from Selene to Athena. "I already know you're going to refuse. But I wonder if you'll still be stubborn if given the right incentive."

"You've got nothing I want," Athena spat.

"Don't I?" He turned and walked to Mom's cage. She was awake, but quiet, her knees drawn to her chest. "The blood work processed overnight. You don't have the same anomaly as your daughters, meaning you're not a lycanthrope and thus expendable."

A chill swept Athena. "Don't you hurt my mom."

"What happens to her will depend on you." He glanced at Athena over his shoulder. "Your choice. Choice A, you show me your wolf. Choice B, you remain stubborn and we see how loud your mom can scream."

"Don't you touch my mommy," Selene shrieked, grabbing the bars.

"I won't have to if you give me what I want."

"Don't listen to him, girls." Mom rose to her feet.

"He can't be trusted. He's going to torture me no matter what."

"I'm hurt." Rogers clutched his chest. "Do you think me a man who'd break his word?"

All three women shouted, "Yes."

His lips curved. "So that's B, then. All right. Let me get the rack and tools ready."

Athena's heart stopped as her mind flashed to her time in the rack. An inversion table with straps. Sturdy ones she couldn't break. He'd had her spread eagle on it numerous times. Unable to block the punches to her body. Unable to stop the slices to her flesh. It had been horrible. But it would be worse this time because it would be her mom suffering.

Rogers walked away and headed upstairs rather than bringing the rack close. Probably grabbing reinforcements.

Mom hissed, "Be strong, girls."

"What's the point? It's only a matter of time before he gets what he wants. Whether today or on the full moon," Athena reminded.

"We just need to hold on."

"For what?" Athena exclaimed. "He's not going to change his mind. He will hurt you. And I don't think I can bear to stand witness."

"Do as mom says," Selene replied. "He won't kill her. He'll lose his leverage."

"He might not kill her, but he will maim." Athena knew his sadistic side. A side she'd tried to forget and that might have played a part in her reneging on her plan for revenge. Fear she'd be his victim again was part of why she chose to remain hiding.

"It will be okay, baby girl. Don't give in." Mom was being so brave, and it killed Athena. The expression on her mom's face was the same as the one she wore at Dad's funeral.

Athena worried more about Selene. While Athena had great control over her wolf side, her sister had to remain calm. When she got too angry, things got hairy. From a young age, their dad had worked with Selene, teaching her to let things slide off her back. It resulted in Selene having a super-positive attitude all the time, even in the midst of calamity. She didn't have a choice. If she were the kind of person who flipped out all the time—wrong amount of sugar in her coffee, person cutting her off in traffic—then her secret would be revealed.

Rogers returned with two guards, or would the better term be mercenaries? They wore no official badges. Didn't have their hair shorn short and sported scruffy jaws. The kind of men who wouldn't bat an eye at torturing a woman.

One of them wheeled over the rack, and Athena couldn't help but tremble. She'd hoped to never see it again.

The mercs entered Mom's cage and grabbed her roughly, despite the fact she didn't fight. Mom shuffled to her fate while Selene and Athena clutched at their bars.

The guards knelt to buckle in her ankles while Rogers handled her left wrist.

"At least one of you understands the futility of resistance," he remarked.

"You'll burn in hell for this," Mom's pleasant reply.

"Hell doesn't exist."

"Neither do werewolves," Mom countered.

"Still sticking to the lie, I see." Rogers went to work on her other hand.

Distant shouting drew Athena's attention. It led to Rogers frowning. He turned to the stocky merc by his side. "Go see what's happening upstairs."

Selene glanced at Athena and mouthed, *Do you hear that?*

Indeed, Athena could hear the distinct pops of gunfire. A shootout? By who? Ares had only one rifle, and surely he wouldn't have come alone to such a guarded place.

Could it be Derek? Unlikely, because, like Ares, he wouldn't know where to find her. Not to mention, only an idiot would go against Rogers and his cadre of goons.

Whatever the case, this could be the distraction they needed to escape.

The walkie at the merc's hip beeped. "What is it?" he barked.

They all heard, "We're under attack."

"Fuck." Rogers eyed the merc. "Go help."

The man trotted, off leaving them with just the doctor.

Selene taunted Rogers. "Sounds like your evil experiment days are over. You're going down."

"Doubtful. My men are armed. You'd need an army—"

Boom!

The structure trembled, as if hit by a mini earthquake. Their cages vibrated, and dust sifted from the ceiling, enough Rogers appeared worried. "Don't move. I'll be right back."

Off he scurried, a roach in a lab coat.

"We should take advantage of this distraction," Selene stated.

"Great idea but we're still behind bars." Athena reminded.

"Hey, Mom." Selene spoke softly. Mom remained strapped to the rack, unharmed for the moment, but that would change the moment Rogers returned. "Can you get your hand loose?"

Rogers hadn't quite finished buckling her in, the flap of the restraint not tucked into the metal loop.

"I don't know." Mom's tongue peeked as she strained and twisted, trying to unlatch.

Selene grabbed her bars and shook. "The tremor didn't loosen mine."

"Mine either," Athena stated, giving them a good tug.

"Hold on, babies, I think I've—Aha!" Mom's hand popped free. "Give me a sec." Mom went to work on her other hand while Athena listened to occasional yell and gunshot. A mini war was being waged, and she could only wonder who had the balls to come after Rogers. Could be rescue, or someone worse.

As Mom bent over to work on her ankles, it seemed like perhaps they'd actually manage to get free.

And then the lights went out.

CHAPTER 15

THE PLANNING TO RESCUE ATHENA, HER MOM, and sister took hours despite the location being only twenty minutes from them. According to Ares' tracking of their chips, they were being kept in an old church, long abandoned but its stone edifice still standing.

"The basement is most likely where they're holding them." Ares pointed to an image he'd found on the internet taken by a drone. Websites that featured abandoned buildings had pictures of the church, inside and out.

"Those stone walls and that front door will be sturdy," Grams noted. "They knew how to build back in the day."

"Bessie won't have a problem plowing through," Gramps asserted.

"Won't that destabilize the structure?" Derek

countered. "If they're in the basement, the whole thing could collapse on them."

"It's a possibility," Ares admitted. "However, we might not have a choice." He pointed to the bell tower. "If we try to approach on foot, a single sniper up here could take us all out before we got close. Not to mention, the plywood over the windows won't come off quietly. I think the element of surprise is our best option, and we'd certainly get that by plowing into the place."

Grams nodded. "If we aim Bessie for the doors and keep her wedged in the opening, it will provide support if the walls try to buckle. So long as Gramps pulls in far enough for me to use my gunner nest, I can provide cover while you two get to the basement and locate the girls."

"By provide cover, you do realize you're talking about killing people," Derek pointed out.

"Not people," Grams spat. "Degenerate assholes who think it's okay to kidnap people."

Derek's lips flattened. "A valid point but, at the same time, I don't want you spending the rest of your life in jail."

"Oh, you sweet bastard. You're assuming that we'll be caught and that anyone will care. If we do this right, we'll rescue the girls and, to cover our tracks, we bomb the place. Bring it down and then toss a bit of gasoline on it before lighting it up to remove all evidence."

"What if someone notices Bessie going to and from

the church?" While Derek wouldn't change his mind about rescuing, putting his grandparents in danger did concern.

"Bessie ain't got plates. Nor a VIN. As far as the government knows, she don't exist. We go in fast; we get out fast," Gramps countered.

They made it sound so easy.

But if they were wrong...

He couldn't think like that. This had to work. They didn't have a choice. The women had to be rescued, and soon. He dreaded to think what might have already happened.

"I need some air." Derek popped outside and sucked in a deep lungful, eyeing the night sky with its twinkling stars.

Ares joined him. "I know the plan's got flaws."

"Ya think? We have no idea how many guards this doctor has or if he will call in law enforcement once we hit the church."

"I doubt the cops will help him."

"He's got connections and money," Derek pointed out.

"He does, but even he's not above the law. Kidnapping people and performing experiments is still highly illegal."

"For all we know it's government sanctioned."

"Any better ideas?"

A sigh left Derek. "No. I know we have to do this,

just like I know people will die. I'm just worried it won't be the bad guys."

"Me too. I wish we had longer to plan. More people to help. Some magical fucking wand. But all my family's got is us."

"Why does this Rogers want you guys so bad? What makes you so special?" Derek glanced at Ares, whose lips flattened.

"What'd Athena tell you?"

"Not much, just that he thought she had interesting genetics."

Ares said nothing for a moment, just gripped the porch rail staring outward before softly saying, "Do you love my sister?"

"Would I be planning an armed assault if I didn't?" his retort.

"Would you love her no matter what? In sickness and health?"

"Duh. What kind of asshole do you take me for?"

"I know you're not, but what I'm about to tell you is kind of fucked up."

"So you do know why Rogers is interested in Athena?"

"Not just her. Me and my sister too. Mom was probably taken by mistake." Ares paused, and his head ducked before he muttered something Derek couldn't hear.

"What was that?"

"I said we're werewolves."

Derek blinked. Processed the claim then laughed. "Fuck off."

"It's true. We inherited the gene from our dad. It's rare all the kids do, but guess we're special."

It took Derek a moment to realize Ares was being quite serious. "Werewolf? As in full moon makes you grow hair and fangs?"

"Yes. Our body changes shape too. Unlike the movies, we're not wolfmen. We turn into actual wolves. My sisters could pass for the regular variety, but with my size, I kind of stand out as a giant."

"Holy shit." Derek wanted to call him a liar. But... he couldn't help but recall Athena's quirks. The leg thumping, the sniffing, the chasing. How she made sure to disappear the night of the full moon. Being a werewolf explained it all except for one thing. "Did your dad bite you?"

"Uh, no?" Ares' nose scrunched in confusion. "Lycans are born, not made."

"That's a relief." Especially considering how many times he and Athena had mixed fluids.

"It's not contagious, and it can even skip generations. My dad's dad didn't have it, but his grandpa did."

"Well, that at least explains Rogers' interest in your family. He wants to expose them for profit and fame."

"Once he does, they're screwed. Even if they aren't kept in some kind of a zoo or lab, they'll never be able to go out in public or live a normal life. They will be ostracized, hounded—"

"Hurt or killed," Derek interjected. People had long feared the monsters in storybooks. He didn't doubt some would feel a need to rid the world of them. "We need to move fast before Rogers gets concrete proof. Guess it's a good thing the full moon isn't for a few weeks."

"We don't have that much time. See, while Athena's got great control over her Lycan side, Selene doesn't. When she gets mad, she wolfs out."

"As in changes without the moon?"

He nodded. "It's why she always tries to be cheerful. Otherwise, if she loses her temper..." Ares exploded his hands.

"Do you think we can succeed?" Derek asked, hoping for honesty because he struggled. Not for himself, but for his grandparents, who insisted on joining them.

"Depends on how many mercenaries he's got running around, as well as other security. I doubt he had time to turn the place into a fortress."

"We need more intel."

"And I know how we can get it. Wanna go for a ride?"

"Where to? To do what?"

"I've got a drone in my truck. We can use it to scout the area. Maybe even get a head count."

"They might spot it," Derek cautioned.

"They might, but it's our best shot at getting the info we need."

"Agreed. I just need to let Grams and Gramps know."

Ares put a hand on his arm before Derek could go inside. "They're pretty awesome, by the way. I don't know many folks their age that would be strapping on guns, offering to drive what is essentially a tank, and going to war for people they don't know."

"They do know Athena and like her. Not to mention, Grams and Gramps have waited their whole life to fight *the man*. You could call this a dream come true for them."

Ares chuckled. "My grandma used to bake cookies, and Grandpa napped all the time. You're lucky."

"I am."

And that worried him. He didn't want to lose them but already knew they'd never stay behind, so he didn't bother trying. Grams would have most likely cuffed him if he had. Instead, he told them they wanted to fly the drone, to which Grams and Gramps nodded but also insisted on coming along in Bessie.

"Might as well tuck ourselves out of sight but close by in case we need to move in fast," Gramps remarked. "She's already loaded with our gear. Just needs one more thing."

That one thing was a bottle of whiskey smashed on her hull to christen her maiden run into battle.

CHAPTER 16

THE ROAD TO THE OLD CHURCH PROVED DARK and empty at this time of night. No traffic, no house, not a single streetlight, which made their headlights all the more noticeable.

He wasn't surprised when Ares pulled over about a kilometer before their destination.

"We'll send up the drone from here."

Bessie, driven by Gramps, rumbled to a stop behind them. Grams stuck her head out. "You flying the bird?"

"Yes, ma'am." Ares had it sitting on the ground with a controller in hand. As he concentrated on getting it into the air and scouting, Derek headed to Bessie to chat with his Grams.

"You sure you two are good to do this?" The bruises on them had blossomed. Grams sported a black eye that had swelled and left it open just a slit.

"Are you really insulting me right now, you little bastard?" she grumbled.

"So sorry. I keep forgetting you're too ornery to die."

Grams inclined her head in Ares' direction. "I like him. Pity we don't have a granddaughter for him to date."

"Well, he still might end up family if things with Athena work out."

"They will," Grams stated with assurance. "After all, wolves mate for life."

His breath stopped. "Er, what?"

"Don't even try to deny it. We heard everything."

Stupid doorbell cam. "You can't tell anyone." Something Ares had stressed on the drive over.

"Duh." Grams rolled her eyes. "As if I'd do anything to jeopardize my future grandbabies."

Babies? "Whoa, you old bat, we're just dating."

"Just?" she snorted. "You're about to go to war for the girl. Just like your gramps did for me."

Gramps grunted. "Would do it again too. And before you ask, boy, the war she's talking about was down in South America. We needed cash, and so we joined a mercenary outfit."

"Wait, what about Dad?"

"Left him with my sister. We was only gone a few months."

"Our first kill was done as a couple." Grams smiled fondly at Gramps. "Remember how he came out of the jungle with that bomb strapped to his chest?"

"Two bullets to the head. Dropped him in his tracks before he could detonate."

The things he'd never known...

Speaking of unknown, it took thirty minutes before Ares returned to report.

"There are two unmarked vans and four cars parked by the old church, around back, out of sight. A generator is back there as well. Outside, I spotted four men patrolling. Two more in the bell tower. I don't know how many inside but counted at least two, who popped out for a smoke."

"So some security but not an insane amount."

"Not surprising," Grams stated. "Too many cars and strange faces in the area would draw attention. Then there's the budget. This doctor had to relocate, which would have cost big bucks. Then there's the salary of those mercenaries. Could be a case of the purse running low."

"Let's hope so, because a dozen men would be a cinch for us to handle, especially if we pick some of them off ahead of time." Ares glanced at Gramps. "How's your aim?"

"You'll want Grams for any sniping. Still has the best shot of the two of us."

"Then why isn't she the one hunting?" Derek asked.

"Because these bones hate the cold and damp.

Speaking of, I've got hot cocoa in a thermos and cookies in a tin. Anyone want a snack?" Grams had a thing about feeding people, apparently even in times of intense stress.

They ate and drank while reviewing the footage. Despite Derek's trepidation, it really did seem as if slamming Bessie through the front door would be their best option for getting inside.

As dawn approached, they readied themselves and ate yet again, as Grams insisted they fill their bellies. She might have been right, since he felt wide awake after. Which led to him eyeing her with suspicion. "What was in those muffins and that protein shake?"

"Why do you ask?"

"Grams..." He injected a warning tone.

"Just a few vitamins and some caffeine... oh and something that I'm not allowed to talk about because it's not technically on the market."

"What the fuck?" he exclaimed.

"I just told you I can't tell you what the fuck it is. Suffice it to say it acts as a bit of an upper. Think of it as a jolt of adrenaline that doesn't wear off for a few hours." Grams grinned.

"Is it safe?" he exclaimed.

"Seemed to work fine for a certain elderly politician." And that was all she'd say.

With the lights turned off, Derek rode once more with Ares, as they would be the ones rushing in after Bessie smashed her way through. Grams had her rifle and scope and sat in the gunner seat, the safety already off the mini mounted machine gun, ready to mow down any opposition, while Gramps drove. They would only exit the vehicle if they had no other choice. Derek had made them promise. Bessie was bulletproof. They weren't.

When Grams pointed out he was made of meat as well, he growled, "If you get killed, I will piss on your grave daily."

"And if you die, you little bastard, I'll never bake cookies again."

Their version of I love you.

As prepared as they could be, they went to war.

Or so it felt.

He and Ares were grim-faced as they neared the old church, rolling slowly in the dark, hoping for the element of surprise, if that was even possible given the growl of the pickup and the even more intense rumble of Bessie.

Soon as they pulled into the church parking lot, overgrown with weeds and even a few saplings pushing through pavement, bright lights turned on, projecting from the bell tower, highlighting them. A voice barked, "You are in a restricted area."

Derek eyed Ares. "If I don't make it, tell Athena I love her, even if she's hairier than me."

Ares' lips quirked. "You'd better make it out alive, or I have a feeling I'll be just as dead as you because my sister will kill me."

The guy on the megaphone still shouted. "Step out of the vehicles with your hands up." Apparently, they were no longer being allowed to leave.

"Showtime," Ares announced, hopping out without a qualm. Derek moved slower. Convinced he'd be shot. Wondering at their madness in thinking they could act as an extraction team. They didn't have the experience or—

Pop.

The guy in the bell tower fired first, the slug embedding in the door of the truck, dropping Derek's jaw. These guys weren't messing around.

Grams shouted, "Fucker, how dare you shoot at my grandson!"

"Surrender now or—" Whoever bellowed in the megaphone cut off mid-sentence as Grams took him out. Either the guy had nerves of steel and didn't scream from his injury, or Grams killed them.

Killed a man.

This was happening.

Holy shit. Derek remained ducked behind the truck's door. He glanced through the cab to Ares crouched on the other side.

Bessie went from idling to moving. Grams' head and shoulders peeked from the hatch in the top as she took aim with her rifle, rather than mowing them down with the mounted machine gun.

Pop. This time someone did yell as they fell from the bell tower. One sniper taken out, but that still left possibly one more and the patrolling guards, who took notice. They hid where they could and began shooting. No one came out of the church, though.

So Bessie went to them.

Crunch. The armored vehicle slammed into the wooden doors, and they tore open, along with part of the stonework. Grams had ducked back into Bessie, but that didn't prevent her from firing with the mounted artillery. *Tika-tika-tika.* She shot at whoever she saw inside. Hopefully not innocents. Please not Athena. They had assumed them stashed in the basement, but what if they were wrong?

Too late now.

Hearing the bang of a gun followed by a grunt, he glanced at Ares. The man had a hand slapped to his shoulder. Blood seeped from under it.

"Fucker shot me." With that, Ares took off running, and Derek cursed. He couldn't leave the guy alone at the same time his grandparents were inside.

Within a bullet-proof truck. Shooting the bad guys.

Ares needed him more.

Derek sprinted around the truck. Of the man, there was no sign, unless the clothes on the ground, wreathed in a rising mist, counted.

The snarl preceded a high-pitched scream, and it took Derek only a second to pinpoint where and then gape. Despite the fog beginning to swirl, he saw the wolf that savaged a man on the ground.

A big fucking wolf.

Like, huge.

Fuck.

Me.

He's.

A.

Werewolf.

Hearing Ares claim it and seeing it? Two different things. It also drove home how important it was to get Athena and her family out of here.

The wolf swung his head and yipped.

While Derek didn't speak canine, it didn't take much to guess what he said.

Get your ass inside and free them.

So much for them going together. Then again, if Ares kept the mercs busy outside, then that was less for Derek to deal with inside the church.

A gun fired, and a bullet dug into the ground by Ares. The wolf sprinted in the direction it came from, the mist swallowing his shape. Derek ran for the church, where weapons still fired.

He slipped in through the opening Bessie created, hugging the side, the settling dust helping to conceal his arrival. The lights strung from the vaulted ceiling showed more people inside than predicted. He counted five bodies and at least a dozen more shooting just on this floor. What did that leave in the basement? Didn't matter. He still had to go.

Unlike his grandparents, Derek had a revolver, not

a rifle, wanting the smaller maneuverability of the weapon especially in close range. While not a sharpshooter like his Grams, he could hit what he aimed at.

His hand was steadier than expected as he gripped the gun. He'd expected to be nervous. Even a bit afraid. After all, this wasn't a fisticuff situation where both parties would walk away. These guys were shooting to kill. If he didn't do the same, he'd die and then Athena, her family, and his family were fucked.

He inched around the outer edge of the room, the dust in the air making it hard to see much. The images they'd studied of the church, with its rotting pews and faded frescoes on the wall didn't resemble the current space. The whole main floor had been cleared for desks and machines. Medical devices, he surmised, seeing some holding vials. The lights on them blinked, motors whirred, and something kept beeping.

There were computers too, the keyboards and their monitors abandoned, most likely when the shooting started.

He saw one woman face down on the floor, shivering in her white coat. Not a mercenary. Just someone working for Rogers. As he crept past, she turned her head and saw him. Her eyes widened.

He tried to give her a reassuring look.

She pushed herself to a sitting position and, to his disbelieving gaze, pulled a gun.

He didn't think; he fired, his shot slightly wild but

still hitting, striking her in the shoulder. She shouted in pain and dropped her weapon.

Grams would probably yell at him, but he didn't fire a finishing bullet.

Instead, he moved faster, heading to the stairs, and ran into his first mercenary. The guy held a gun and stood guard at the top of the staircase, his goggles hiding his eyes, a gaiter covering the lower half of his face. He looked a lot like a bad guy in one of his video games, making it easier this time to take aim and fire.

The merc went down without firing his gun, and a moment later, Derek had his foot on the first step.

Which was when the lights went out.

CHAPTER 17

THE LIGHTS WENT OUT, AND WITH THE LACK of humming machinery, the silence deafened. The shooting also stopped for the moment.

"Mom?" Athena called out to her.

"Still here, baby girl. Almost got my feet untied." A hiss and Mom exclaimed, "I'm loose, but I can't see a darned thing."

"Follow my voice." Athena began talking. "Just walk slow, hands in front of you so you don't smash your face into anything."

"What's happening?" Mom asked.

"Ares came for us," Selene replied.

"How did he know where to find us?" Athena asked.

"I couldn't say anything before because of the cameras, but he GPS-chipped us when you went missing. Thought he was a little nuts at the time but turned out he had the right idea."

"Chipped?" Athena didn't even know that was possible.

"Think of it as an air tag for humans, only it's inside our bodies."

"Well, damn." No wonder Selene appeared so confident about rescue.

"Athena?"

Mom sounded close, and Athena murmured, "Not far now, Mom. Just a few more steps." She heard rather than saw the hand that slapped into her bars. "You found me. Now feel for the lock." The doctor hadn't used electronic ones this time but rather good old-fashioned padlocks.

"How am I supposed to open it? I don't have a key."

"Fuck." For some reason, Athena had forgotten that crucial component. "Maybe you can smash it."

"With what?" her mother huffed. "Dammit. I wish I could see. Let me go groping and see what I can find." Mom wandered off, her feet sliding on the floor.

Selene sighed. "We're so dumb. Rogers has the key."

"I'm aware." Her ears caught a sound. "Someone's coming. Hide, Mom." Kind of an oxymoron since none of them could see shit.

The person coming down had a heavy step, but it

wasn't until she heard, "Athena?" that she relaxed, and her heart burst.

"Derek!"

"Thank fuck. Are you all right?" he exclaimed.

"Yes, but me and my sister are stuck in a cage."

"What about your mom? Is she here too?" he asked.

"I'm here," Mom chirped. "You must be the man Athena was blushing about."

"Mom!" Athena felt her cheeks heating and was glad Derek couldn't see.

"What? It's true. Never seen you do that before," Mom retorted.

"Hello, ma'am. What do you say we get out of here so we can actually meet?" Amusement hued Derek's words.

"I was looking for something to smash the locks," Mom explained. "Rogers has the key."

"I can help with that. Athena, where are you?"

"Over here, honey. I take it Ares recruited you?"

"Yeah, he showed up at the farm looking for you and told us what happened to your sister and mom. Sorry we didn't get here sooner. We had to scout the situation first to make sure we didn't fail in our rescue."

"Are your grandparents okay? Rogers and his goons attacked them."

"They're fine and in their glory. I've never seen

them so excited. Gramps has been hoping he'd have a chance to use Bessie before he died."

"Bessie?"

"Bessie is an armored vehicle he's been tinkering on for years. Think of it as a Mad-Max truck made for the apocalypse."

"Hold on. He's here?"

"Grams too." His voice sounded close. "Who do you think is holding off Rogers' men?"

Selene started laughing. "Oh my God, you didn't mention how cool his family was."

"Very cool, with the exception of his ass of a cousin," Athena muttered.

"Grams almost killed Frank. She still might after this," Derek replied from right in front. Close enough that when she ran her fingers over the bars, she found his hands.

He clasped them tight and whispered, "I'm so sorry I wasn't there, sugarplum."

"You're here now. You couldn't have known."

"You sure you're okay?"

"I'll be better once I'm out of this fucking cage," she grumbled.

"Stand back while I shoot the lock."

Athena shuffled to the back of the cage, and her ears vibrated when he fired.

"Hold on while I... Got it. Come on," Derek ordered.

"Coming. Help my sister. She's right across from me."

He slipped away, and she aimed for the front of her cage, her hands feeling to find the opening and stepping out.

Bang.

Selene crowed, "Freedom!"

"You and that movie," Athena huffed but good-naturedly. Maybe they would escape this place alive.

Maybe...

They'd yet to see the situation outside the basement. While no guns fired, that didn't mean shit.

"Mom?"

"Right here, baby girl."

She sensed her mom a second before her hands clutched her arm. "Selene? Derek?"

"I've got your sister," Derek replied. "Let's head back upstairs. Stay behind me."

"Chivalrous too, lucky girl," Selene murmured.

"Paws off my man," Athena muttered, to which her sister laughed.

Her sister clung to Mom, who shuffled between them as they made their way to the stairs, Derek leading the way and cursing when he bumped his foot. "Shift left. There's something in the way."

They followed his instructions and made it across the room.

"Where are we?" Athena whispered.

"Abandoned church basement. Watch your step. The stairs are straight ahead."

He crept up first, while Athena hung back with her mom and sister, even as she itched to be by his side. This wasn't his fight, yet he'd volunteered, him and his grandparents. It boggled the mind they would risk themselves for her, a person they'd known a month.

It took a moment to realize she could see. The lightening proved gradual, pitch-black turning gray, and moist.

"A fog's rolled in," he murmured. The morning mist was common in fall when the warmer ground hit the cooler air.

They emerged from the stairwell into what she assumed to be a cavernous space from feeling alone, not one she could truly see with the lights off and the moist air kissing her skin.

It was quiet, too quiet, and Derek muttered, "Bessie's not running."

"Is that bad?" she whispered back.

"Hope not. Stick close. Everyone hold on to each other. I'm going to bring us in the direction of the door." She hooked her fingers to the loops in his pants, leaving his hands free even as she wanted to clutch one. Mom grabbed hold of the hem of Athena's shirt, and she assumed Selene did the same to her mom.

They shuffled, their feet sliding and sounding much too loud. Every so often her foot would nudge something soft and squishy, a body, but the kicking of something that rattled as it rolled had Derek hissing, "Fuck."

"Is that you, little bastard?" Grams suddenly yelled.

"Yeah, it's me, you old coot. I've got Athena and family. What's the situation?"

"I think the church is empty. Hard to tell with the lights out and this fucking fog," Grams complained. "Should have brought the goggles."

"Did you get Rogers?" Athena called out.

"I don't think so. The men I shot weren't wearing white coats. He could be hiding in the back office."

"He can't be allowed to leave," Athena stated. If he escaped, then they'd have to live in fear he'd come back.

Derek murmured, "Let's get your mom and sister to Bessie, and then we'll see if we can hunt him down."

"If he's not already left," her ominous reply.

"I doubt your brother would have allowed that."

"Where is Ares?" she asked, surprised he'd not been inside as part of the rescue.

"Handling the guards outside. I think he took out the generator, too."

Smart.

A pair of lights illuminated, diffused by the fog but giving them a direction. It meant they didn't trip on the shattered equipment and could step over the prone bodies. Once they reached the source of the lights, she could see Bessie, and she turned out to be exactly as Derek described, a futuristic armored truck with a grinning Gramps in the driver's seat. Grams hung out at the top, gray hair peeking, looking a tad demonic with her wide grin and rifle in hand.

"Get in through the passenger door," Grams called out. "There's cocoa and tea in the thermoses, as well as snacks if you're hungry."

"Thank you," Mom exclaimed. "Thank you so much, Gertie. From now on, all your honey is on the house."

It took a second for Athena to realize that was Grams' real name.

"Bah. I should be paying you. This is the most fun I've had in years. Get in. Get in. We're going to be reversing shortly and blowing this place to pieces. Gotta hide the evidence."

Athena approved of that plan. While some of Rogers' research might remain on a hard drive somewhere, the samples would at least be destroyed.

Mom and Selene wasted no time getting inside Bessie, but Athena didn't join them. She wasn't done hunting.

"This way." Derek held her hand while the other one gripped a gun. He led her outside into a world of swirling mist. In the open, it hung so thick she could barely see Derek by her side.

It muffled sound as well, and strain as she might, she struggled to hear anything. She'd never find Rogers in this.

Grawr. The sudden growl of a wolf and a man

yelling, "Where is it?" had her moving fast and instantly tripping, as the uneven pavement caught at her feet.

Derek hauled her up before she hit the ground. "Move slower," he cautioned. "Won't help your brother much if you twist an ankle, or worse."

She inched, chafing at her slow speed, but Derek was right. She couldn't allow something stupid to stop her from helping her brother.

"I see him, argh!" A man screamed as the sounds of growling intensified.

A sudden yelp made Athena flinch.

"I got him!" someone crowed. "Shoot him with another tranq. He's not going down." The same man screamed as the snarling continued.

She flinched at each *pft* sound of the dart being fired. Poor Ares.

"He's down!" crowed someone she couldn't yet see.

"Take him to the car." Athena stiffened as Rogers barked the command, his voice unmistakable. The fucker lived and appeared to have captured Ares.

"We have to stop them," she huffed.

"They're parked around back," Derek said just as an engine roared to life.

The direction led to her slapping a hand on the church and using it to guide her through the thick fog. As she turned the corner, she was in time to see two glowing eyes in the mist.

Not eyes, headlights.

"They're getting away!"

"No, they're not," Derek's grim reply. He aimed and fired, the popping of a tire explosively loud. Another shot and the engine whined before dying.

Car doors opened with Rogers shouting, "Shoot them." Shots pinged from the mist, flying wildly, as they couldn't see each other. A good thing for them.

"We need to reach that vehicle," she huffed.

"I'll cover you. Stay low," Derek advised.

As he fired back, someone screamed, "I'm hit! Oh, God."

Athena crouched low and ran in a zigzag for the vehicle, the fog making her difficult to spot. The pavement here hadn't buckled as bad, and she managed to not trip.

When she suddenly came face to face with an armed man, she couldn't say who was more surprised.

"Duck!" Derek yelled from closer than expected.

She dropped. So did the guy when the bullet took him in the chest.

Having reached the rumbling van, she rounded the open driver-side door and found a body on the ground, bled out from the nick at his neck. She peeked in to see the front seats empty, but in the back...

A very big and unconscious wolf.

Ares... Oh shit. How to hide this from Derek?

There was no time. Derek was by her side and saw the wolf. "Don't panic. Your brother's alive," he stated, running his hands over Ares' flanks. "A few injuries but nothing that can't be patched."

He knew.

"You're okay with..." She waved a hand at her brother's furry shape.

His lips quirked. "It was a bit of a shock hearing about it, but it explains a lot. Although I will go on the record now saying if you sniff my butt, I am not responsible for what you smell."

Her laughter sounded out of place. "Fair enough." She turned from the van. "The doctor's not in the truck."

"He can't have gotten far." Derek squinted at the fog.

"Which direction, though?" She scanned best she could, but in this shape, her senses of hearing, sight, and most especially smell were greatly reduced.

If she were a wolf, though...

She glanced at Derek. Would he notice her slipping away?

"What's wrong?"

"I need to find Rogers. If he escapes, then we'll need to disappear. Which is fine for us, but Mom won't want to leave the farm."

"This fog is too thick," he grumbled.

"For human senses, yes."

"Do it." He understood right away.

"You won't be freaked out?"

"Depends. You going to tear my face off?"

"Nah. You're cute. Although I might bite other parts." She waggled her brows.

His lips quirked. "You should get going before Rogers gets too far."

"Okay. Maybe look away?"

He turned around, and she quickly stripped, tossing her clothes in the van to keep them from the damp ground. Then she had to concentrate. Unlike her brother, she needed to drop into an almost Zen-like state when trying to shift without the full moon.

It took a few calming breaths.

In.

Out.

Then it happened, the sprout of fur, the rearrangement of her bones and muscles. When she landed on the ground on four paws, it was to find Derek watching, his lips in a rueful twist.

"Sorry, curiosity got the better of me."

She barked.

"Still going to bang you, although the term doggy-style just took on new meaning."

She chuffed.

"I'll be pestering you with questions later, but right now... can you track the doctor?"

She padded around the van, sniffing, finding the scent she hated by the passenger side door. Cologne, antiseptic, and pure asshole.

With a yip, she began trotting, the mist obscuring her view, but scent didn't lie. She followed the trace of it, heading out of the parking lot into the overgrown cemetery, the gravestones abrupt sentinels in the mist. Rogers had slammed into one in his flight.

The doctor made it across the boneyard into the field beyond, the shorn cornstalks crunchy if brushed, but even better, they crackled loudly when stepped on by a man in shoes, giving her sound to follow while her paws navigated them silently.

A low muttered, "Fuck me, where's the road?" had her tail wagging. Rogers was right ahead.

And then the doctor was in front of her, a bulky form that parted the mist and provided a perfect target. She leaped and knocked him to the ground, snarling.

To her surprise, he proved stronger than expected, heaving her from his body before standing.

She scrambled to four paws and kept low as she growled, stalking him.

The fucker sighed. "You just couldn't cooperate, could you? You do realize even if you kill me, all my notes, everything I've catalogued remains on my hard drive. This won't save you."

No, but she'd sure feel good about it.

"Why not collaborate with me instead? I could make you famous."

"In a cage?" Derek appeared from the mist, gun cradled in his hands. "She's not an animal."

"Says the guy willfully ignoring what's in front of him," Rogers scoffed. "She and her siblings are monsters."

"I only see one monster here, and it's not wearing fur," Derek snapped.

"How can you be so blind? Look at her. A savage beast. Do you really want a dog as the mother of your children?"

"Whoa. We're not even engaged yet. And even if we were having kids, do you really think I'd care? Happy and healthy. That's all that matters."

"Until they hurt someone."

"Hurt who?" Derek scoffed. "The only one causing harm is you."

While Derek talked, Athena inched closer. Might have even gotten a clean kill if Rogers didn't suddenly lunge, a dart in hand, which he used to jab down. The sharp tip pierced her skin and fur, drawing a yelp.

Derek didn't fuck around.

He shot Rogers in the head.

A single shot to end the nightmare.

CHAPTER 18

DEREK THOUGHT HE'D FEEL WORSE ABOUT killing someone in cold blood. But hearing Rogers, and knowing what he'd done and would continue to do... It felt good to remove that kind of evil from the world.

Not so fun? Carting back the dead body to the church. He couldn't exactly leave it for people to find.

Bessie rumbled outside the church, becoming visible as the morning sun burned away the mist.

Selene and her mom did their best to haul a body lying outside into the building, one holding the head, the other the feet, but both huffed with strain. Grams and Gramps might be old, but years of working a farm left them strong. They each dragged one inside. Derek knew better than to tell them to sit down while he handled it.

Derek dumped Rogers within before exiting to give Selene and her mom a hand. "I've got this."

"Thank you," Athena's mom murmured. "For everything."

"Ares is in a van at the back having a nap if you want to check on him."

The women scurried off, as did Athena still in fur, trotting around the church. Only when she was out of sight did Grams whistle. "Fine-looking wolf. Glad we got here in time."

"You okay with my girlfriend being a werewolf?" he asked. Not that it mattered. He couldn't change how he felt.

"Are you kidding? I'm going to have the most epic great-grandbabies ever!" Grams exclaimed.

Whereas Gramps rumbled, "We'll need a few extra freezers to store meat once they learn to hunt."

Figured his grandparents would focus on the positive. And he knew he could trust them to keep the secret.

"You're sure this will burn all the evidence of what they were doing?"

"Yup. The bones might be found, but the cops will assume a drug lab gone kaboom." Grams pointed to a case in the back of Bessie. "You just need to plant this meth in one of the vehicles they were using."

"Do I dare ask how you got the meth?"

"Drugs will be excellent for trading once the apocalypse hits."

He held in a sigh. She did have a point.

It took less time than expected to move all the

bodies and plant the drugs. Ares got moved from the van to his truck bed, where he continued to snooze.

When it came time to light the fire, Grams offered the Molotov cocktail and lighter to Athena—who'd shifted and dressed while they cleared the scene.

"Would you do the honors?"

"With pleasure," Athena stated.

She lit the rag and tossed it perfectly inside the broken doorway. Flames immediately whooshed, the gasoline inside igniting.

They didn't stay to watch it burn. Better to be far away before someone noticed and the fire crews came to put it out.

The call for Derek to go in and fight it came just as they pulled into the driveway. Derek almost called in sick, but this was his chance to ensure they'd not forgotten anything.

So back out he went, taking his gramps' pickup, joining up with the fire crew who could do little but ensure the church fire didn't spread.

The vehicles closest got singed pretty good, but the van with drugs remained intact enough for the cops to declare it a drug lab operation.

When one of them spotted blood on the pavement, the theory went from meth lab explosion to drug war. Or as the detective stated, "Looks like a rival gang wiped them out. Good news in a sense for the taxpayer, as dead criminals are cheaper than live ones awaiting trial."

By the time he made it back to the farm, Derek ached with exhaustion. Upon walking in, he expected to be bombarded with questions and chaos, but instead only Athena waited.

"Where is everyone?" he asked.

"Out for dinner. Your Grams thought you might need some peace and quiet."

"I do." He sighed.

"Do you need me to leave?"

"Fuck no!" He dragged her close in a hug that left no room for argument. "Everyone's okay?"

She nodded against his chest, remaining snuggled. "Ares woke up pissed he missed the ending. Selene and Mom are fine. Your grandparents are rockstars."

"Yeah, they are," he agreed.

"Grams left you some venison stew. Delicious by the way."

Hearty as well, it did much to revive him after he had two bowls.

But what really put a spring in his step?

"Let's get you clean. Come on, shower time."

Whatever fatigue plagued him vanished when he realized she would be joining him.

She stripped him then herself before getting him to stand under the hot spray.

The hot water felt good on his tired muscles but not as good as her slippery hands sliding over his body with the soap. He squinted at her through the spray.

"I don't know how much stamina I've got left, sugarplum."

"How about you let me do the work?" she said with a wink.

She sank down in the tub, crouching to put herself face level with his cock.

A cock that wasn't too tired to rise.

She gripped his shaft with soapy fingers and began to pull and stroke.

Damn that felt good. His head leaned back as he sighed and let her play.

"Turn," she ordered.

He rotated, and she kept her fingers on him as she rinsed him clean then tugged at his hips to turn him away from the spray. But his dick didn't get dry, not with her mouth suddenly enveloping it.

"Oh." That was the only syllable he could grunt as she worked his cock with her mouth, sliding her lips up and down the length of his shaft, taking him to the back of her throat, suctioning him, teasing him with the graze of her teeth.

He braced a hand against the shower wall as she sucked him and made his knees weak. He moaned as she hollowed her cheeks and teased the tip. His hips thrust in time to her cadence, and he felt his balls tightening.

"Better stop or you'll be getting a salty surprise," his raspy warning.

"Mmm. So tempting." She kept sucking.

"I'd rather fuck you," his blunt reply. "I wanna come inside you. Wanna feel you squeezing around me as you orgasm."

She shuddered and paused, looking up at him, her eyes smoldering with lust. "Way to make it impossible for me to refuse."

His lips quirked. "Good. Shall we go to bed?"

"And get the sheets all wet?" She shook her head. "Let's do it in the shower." With that, she bent over, ass tilted, legs spread, showing off her pink pussy.

Fuck...

He dragged his fingers across her wet slit, parting her lips, feeling the heat and wetness that awaited.

Her ass wiggled. "You going to look at it all day or fuck it?"

"Can't I do both?" he replied.

"No. I need you. Now."

No man alive would have refused that demand.

The tip of his shaft teased her sex, pressing between her lips, feeling the welcoming tightness of her pussy. He grabbed hold of her hips to keep her steady as she slid into her. Fuck she was so perfect. Snug. Clenching.

Bouncing.

She rocked on her heels, shoving herself against him, driving him deeper. "Fuck me," she panted. "Fuck me good."

You'd think by now he'd be used to her dirty talk. Used to her flipping between wanting soft and sensual to hard pounding. Each time it drove him a little crazy.

In a good way.

He gave her what she wanted. Pounded into her willing flesh. Thrust fast, deep, hard. His fingers dug into her flesh as he ground into her, driven by her mewling cries. The suction on his cock got tighter, and he began to grind, just angling his hips, over and over, feeling her tighten and tighten.

"Oh fuck yes," she huffed as she came.

A ripple of her muscles that had him gasping and exclaiming, "I fucking love you."

He did.

There was no other woman he would have killed a man for.

No other woman who completed him so perfectly.

No one else he wanted to spend his life with until they were both wrinkled and old.

When their climax subsided, he dragged her into his arms, holding her tight under the warm spray, which turned cold.

"Yikes!" She hopped out of the shower and grabbed the towel. The only towel apparently.

"You gonna share that?"

She eyed the fabric around her body then him before whipping it off and, with an impish smile, handing it over, saying, "Yeah, I'll share, but only because I love you."

After that, it was like they couldn't stop. They

cuddled in bed, murmuring their plans for a future, pretending as if tomorrow would be an awesome day.

Maybe it would. So long as the cops didn't look too deep. But he knew there would be questions. The vehicles would lead to the owners. The owners would lead to Dr. Rogers. At which point their attempt to play with the crime scene would fall apart.

Hopefully by the time that happened, he, Athena, and her family would be long gone. He'd leave with her when they fled. They'd build a new life together somewhere. He'd miss his grandparents, but he couldn't walk away from the love he had for Athena.

He hoped Grams and Gramps understood.

They fell asleep entwined and woke together, stretching and touching, smiling like idiots. They were still grinning when they went downstairs to the sound of pots rattling and the smell of frying bacon.

They walked into a kitchen full of people. Family to be exact. Grams at the stove, Athena's mom by her side, giving a hand. Selene sat by Gramps, and her hands moved as she talked. Ares sat on the floor with the dog's head in his lap. A dog that no longer raised hackles when Athena went near.

"Morning," Derek murmured.

A chorus of mornings chirped back in reply. It was Athena who frowned and said, "Why does everyone look like they ate the canary?"

"Don't you mean rabbit? Canaries aren't even a snack," Ares riposted.

Athena arched a brow. "What did you do?"

"What makes you think I did anything?"

"Because I know that smug look. You're awfully pleased with yourself."

Ares shrugged. "I am, but can't take the credit. This genius lady over there deserves it."

That led to Derek now frowning and saying, "Grams? What did you do?"

"Well, as we were having dinner last night, it occurred to me that the cops, even if mostly incompetent, might figure out Rogers was at that church, which would then lead them to his home, a home that might have things best left undiscovered."

Derek pursed his lips. "Don't tell me you blew up his house."

"Oh no. That wouldn't have been very nice, given his close neighbors. But we did pay it a visit."

"To do what?" Athena asked.

Selene took over. "Well, first we wiped his hard drives of all info on the lycanthropy project. You can thank Gramps for that. The man is a whiz at cracking into computers."

"Gramps?" Derek blinked.

"Bah, I like puzzles. Wasn't that hard. The idiot had his password in code on his desk. Wasn't too hard to figure out." Gramps downplayed the effort.

"Once we got into his computer, it was easy-peasy wiping the lycan stuff entirely, putting in some meth-related material, a bit of underage porn, oh, and a trail that showed him money-laundering the government funds he'd been allocated." Selene grinned.

"We also busted open his safe, which held some backup drives. We took those, along with his passport, cash, and a suitcase of clothes," Ares added.

"Making it look like he fled," Athena murmured.

Left unsaid, making Rogers look guilty.

"You forgot the part where I had to leave my rifle," Grams groused. "My favorite rifle."

"Which left many holes in the bodies at the church," Ares reminded. "Forensics will match them up and go looking for its owner."

"Which isn't me. The beauty of unregistered firearms." Then to Grams... "I'll get you a new one. A better one!" Gramps declared.

Grams smirked. "You'll regret that. You know which one I've had my eye on."

Gramps offered a rare smile. "I do. And you deserve it. That was some fine shooting."

"You did all that last night?" Athena squeaked.

"Well yeah. Had to be done before the cops showed up," Ares pointed out.

"Won't they realize Rogers is one of the bodies?" Derek wanted to believe this would work, but he couldn't take chances.

"Not without dental records for him they won't," Selene chirped. "Unfortunately, a pipe above his dentist office burst. Ruined everything, and wouldn't you know, they were too cheap to back up off-site."

"Sounds like you thought of everything," Athena replied.

"We sure did. I couldn't have the little bastard running off with you," Grams snapped.

"Why, Grams, would you have missed me?"

To his surprise, she eyed him and muttered, "Yeah, I would have. But don't let it go to your head. Enough of this mushy bullshit. Everyone sit. It's time to eat."

The mood proved exuberant, the chatter lively, a big ol' family breakfast of which he hoped to have many.

Athena sat by his side, occasionally squeezing his leg, stealing his bacon, laughing.

They'd survived. They were in love.

As for the fact his girlfriend was a werewolf? The sky was the limit when it came to canine jokes and gifts.

And when she kissed him later on in the hall, her foot thumping madly, he was never happier because, as Grams told him, wolves mated for life.

EPILOGUE

DEREK SPENT THE EVENING OF THE FULL MOON playing cards with Athena's mom, a true shark. He lost all his Smarties by the time they went to bed. Not that he slept much. He waited for Athena, who returned at dawn after spending the night wolfing out with her siblings.

"Hi, honey," she murmured as she crawled into bed.

"Come here." He grabbed her and snuggled her close. Relieved she'd made it through another shift. It had been almost two months since the whole thing with Rogers went down, but he still worried, even as no one came close to guessing the truth.

There'd been much shock in the news—and on social media—when the events of the church unfolded. A drug lab, run by the renowned doctor who'd double-crossed his people and fled with a ton of money. The cops had bought the story they planted, and even better, with the doctor discredited, things improved for the Sasquatch in custody. Fred's vocal proponents managed to have the courts declare him sentient and, as such, got the Bigfoot released. The Ogopogo remained a tourist attraction in its lake. However, the animal activists had improved its living conditions.

Not a word was ever said about werewolves. No one ever came knocking—although Grams and Gramps kept a close eye, even upping their security.

Frank got arrested for embezzlement and was in jail awaiting trial.

Grams and Athena's mom collaborated and created a THC-infused honey that was selling like hotcakes as people snatched it up as Christmas presents and for personal use.

He and Athena had moved into their own place but spent most of their weekends at one farm or the other.

Derek had never been happier, a happiness that trebled when Athena suddenly lurched from bed and ran to the bathroom to puke. And before anyone thought him a jerk for not following, Athena didn't like having her hair held while she barfed.

When she returned, he arched a brow. "Still think it was that sushi?"

Her wry smile said it all. "Guess it's a good thing we rented a two bedroom." Because, by this time next year, there'd be a little person crawling—or trotting—around.

"I love you," he stated. More than he could ever imagine.

"Prove it," she said as she crawled back into bed.

"How? Massage? The best oral of your life? Name it, and it's yours."

"I want ice cream. Make that a sundae. With whipped cream and bananas."

"It's six a.m.," he reminded.

"And?"

"Anything for you."

And he meant it. Now and always.

————————

ARES UNLOADED THE TREES HE'D CUT AND bound for the Christmas Market. While they used to allow people to come and choose their own at the farm, there'd been too many incidents with idiots who didn't listen to instructions and proved scary with an axe. Much better to provide them ready to go at the market. Quick money that he'd use to spoil his mother and sisters. A little extra would be nice, too, given Athena looked to be expecting a child with her firefighter boyfriend. Not that she'd announced it, but Ares smelled the change in her during their moon run.

196

As Ares whirled from his leaning stack to grab another tree, he startled at the sight of a little girl eyeballing him.

Rosy-cheeked, eyes bright. Her woolen red hat and mittens didn't match her light blue snowsuit at all.

"Hi," chirped the kid.

"Hey."

"Your trees are squished," she observed.

"They'll fluff out nice once we undo the twine."

The child cocked her head. "Mama says real trees are messy."

"Sometimes, but they sure smell good." Good enough he'd apparently pissed on them when he was little with no regard for the fact they sat in the living room. Drove his mom nuts, whereas Dad always laughed and claimed, *"Boy's just marking his territory."*

"Greta, you better not be bugging that man," a woman called out as she bustled over, her bright pink earmuffs holding back her dirty-blonde hair.

"He has real trees, Mommy." Greta pointed. "They're squishy now, but he says they smell good and get fluffy. Can we have one?"

"We are not getting a tree, sweet pea."

The tyke's lips turned down. "I know. 'Cause we need food and not fri-vol-ussy things."

Ares found himself tightening as the child inadvertently revealed the real reason mom didn't have one.

"One day, I'll get you the biggest tree you ever

197

saw," the woman murmured as she crouched by the child.

"Okay." Greta didn't have a tantrum like some kids.

Mom leaned close to whisper, "I saw a snowman wandering."

"Snowmen can't walk," snorted the kid.

"Well, this one is, and he has candy canes!"

"Ooooh." Greta glanced left and right before spotting the suited character. "I see him!" She bolted for the snowman with candy.

The woman rose. "Sorry if she disturbed you."

"Nah, she was fine. Cute kid."

"Precocious with no filter you mean."

His lips curved. "She is. She mentioned you guys don't have a tree. Why don't you take one, on the house?"

She eyed him, her expression suspicious at the offer. "I don't need your charity."

"Hardly charity. I already know I won't sell all of these. So you taking one now saves me carting it back to my place."

Her lips pursed. "While your offer is kind, I'm afraid I don't have a way to get it to our place. But thank you."

With that, the pretty woman headed for her daughter, and Ares found himself glancing at her often as she strolled the Christmas Market. Not buying anything, but managing to give her kid a fun afternoon of face painting, a visit from Santa, and, of course, a fistful of candy canes.

When Ares closed up, toting five trees back onto the trailer he'd used to haul them, he noticed a red mitten lying on the ground. A woolen one he recognized and, stitched inside, a name.

Greta Dawson.

The kid would need it with snow in the forecast and mom tight on dough.

Hunting down where Greta and her mom lived wasn't stalking but rather doing a good deed. It wasn't hard. Not many Dawsons in the area.

One to be exact.

The townhome, which probably hadn't seen better years since it had been built fifty years ago, looked tidy compared to its neighbors. The walkway clear of snow and ice. A wreath that had obviously been made by a child hanging on the door. The front window plastered in paper cut-out snowflakes.

Ares knocked and stood waiting.

When the door flung open, the woman exclaimed, "What are you doing here?"

He held up the mitten. "I found this."

Before the woman could reply, there was a blood-curdling scream from inside.

The woman turned and bolted inside the house.

Ares didn't think. He followed.

EVE LANGLAIS

ARE YOU READY FOR THE NEXT BOOK? *MY BOYFRIEND MARKS
TREES.*

200